	A	B	C	D	E	F	G	H
		638	72	09	32	97	13	08
						96	24	17
							85	

	I	J	K	L	M	N	P	Q
	69		74			38		
	87							
	95							

SPECIAL NEEDS UNIT   01902 556256

THE TOFF AND THE KIDNAPPED CHILD

The Honourable Richard Rollison, aka 'The Toff', is called in to investigate the disappearance of Ralph Kane. But, before the night is out, word comes that beautiful, wealthy Mrs Kane's daughter is also missing.

Caroline is sixteen, a charming girl popular with everyone at her boarding-school. Miss Abbott, her housemistress, has no doubt that Caroline meant to keep her word and come straight back from Hapley station that evening. And yet she did not return.

Rollison drives the distraught Mrs Kane on a midnight journey to the school, his sense of urgency almost equalling hers, for this second disappearance seems even graver than the first . . .

THE TOFF AND THE KIDNAPPED CHILD

John Creasey

First published 1960
by
Hodder & Stoughton

This edition 2006 by BBC Audiobooks Ltd
published by arrangement with
Tethered Camel Publishing

ISBN 10: 1 4056 8540 9
ISBN 13: 978 1 405 68540 5

British Library Cataloguing in Publication Data available

Printed and bound in Great Britain by
Antony Rowe Ltd., Chippenham, Wiltshire

CONTENTS

Chapter		Page
1	REQUEST FOR HELP	7
2	THE SECOND DISAPPEARANCE	15
3	NIGHT JOURNEY	25
4	WARNING	33
5	GUILTY FATHER?	43
6	JEFF	50
7	SECOND NOTE	57
8	KENSINGTON 33412	66
9	REASON TO KILL	73
10	TRUTH?	80
11	COSY LITTLE CHAT	88
12	THE BROTHERS	96
13	STALEMATE	104
14	£20,000	113
15	REPORT	120
16	BLAME?	128
17	RALPH KANE	137
18	MOOD TO KILL	144
19	CHOICE	152
20	SPEED	160
21	FAIR EXCHANGE?	168
22	MAX GLOATS	178
23	PARTING	186

1

REQUEST FOR HELP

ROLLISON was sitting in a deep arm-chair, reading Gustav Schenk's *Book of Poisons* with awed fascination, when the front door bell rang. It was late for an unexpected caller, nearly ten o'clock, and he lifted his eyes from the book and listened for any sound from Jolly, his man. Jolly seemed to have some kind of gastric flu, and had been advised to go to bed early; but a footstep came almost at once, which proved that he had ignored advice; that was usual, if to follow it meant causing Rollison inconvenience.

There was a passage leading from the domestic quarters to the lounge hall of his Mayfair flat; and a door, ajar, leading from the hall to the living-room. Rollison felt compulsively drawn towards a vivid description of the mushrooms which could make men drunk, less compulsively drawn to guess who had called. The front door opened. Rollison felt a momentary qualm, because unexpected callers had been known to come possessed with the thought of violence, his reputation being what it was.

Jolly's voice reassured him.

"Good evening, madam." His voice and the 'madam' made it clear that the caller was a stranger. Forgetting intoxicating mushrooms, Rollison leaned his head on the back of the chair, and listened intently for any vocal clue to the caller's identity.

"Good evening. Is Mr Rollison in?" It was a pleasant voice, that of a cultured woman, not put on.

"I will find out if you care to wait a moment," Jolly said. "What name may I tell him, please?"

"I am Mrs Kane."

"Thank you, madam." Jolly's voice gave away more

7

than the woman's; he liked the look of her. The front door closed, there was a rustle of the evening newspaper which Jolly always kept available for any caller whom Rollison might not want to see at once. Jolly walked audibly towards his own quarters and the kitchen, and a moment later came in at the other door of the large, well-proportioned room on the top floor of a graceful terrace house.

He kept his voice low. "A Mrs Kane has called, sir."

"And you think I ought to see her," Rollison hazarded.

"I think you would wish to, sir."

"You shall be the judge," said Rollison, resignedly. "How are your aches and pains?"

"A little easier, sir."

"Good. Don't go too far away, in case you're wrong. It might be wise to have a witness to what our caller says," observed Rollison, out of bitter experience.

"Very good, sir," said Jolly.

He bowed slightly, turned, and went to the lounge-hall door. Rollison smiled at his back, as ever mildly amused because Jolly was so very much what he should be: the gentleman's gentleman of the past behaving as if there were no social differences between past and present. Rollison stood up, closed the *Book of Poisons* and left it on the arm of his chair, and went to his desk. This was a large pedestal one of figured walnut, inlaid with Spanish leather, and behind it was what had become known and almost legendary as his Trophy Wall. This was adorned with souvenirs of the many crimes he had investigated, and the adornments helped to explain his own momentary qualm. Not many months ago a man had called about this time on a blustery March evening, with the avowed intention of shooting Rollison; he had been the son of a man recently freed after spending nearly ten years in prison at Rollison's instigation. Apparently the father had told the son that only Rollison had been to blame for catching him out in violent crime.

The door opposite the desk opened, and Jolly murmured: "Mrs Kane, sir," and stood aside.

One glance was sufficient to tell Rollison why Jolly had been so well disposed. It was not that the woman was beautiful, as beauty went; she was somehow exactly 'right'. She was quite tall, slim without being thin, and on this warm July evening she wore a linen suit with dusty yellow flowers on a green background. She wore a yellow hat with a fairly large brim, which wasn't ridiculously like a halo. She had yellow gloves, too, all the yellows matching perfectly, and she carried a brown crocodile handbag and a small umbrella which dangled from her left arm. Suit, accessories and make-up were all the same: of quality. A little more dark hair showed on the right of her face than the left, because the hat was slightly tilted. She was grave. She had very fine, clear blue eyes, and in them there was curiosity and probably anxiety. She looked only at Rollison, and she did not appear to notice the remarkable wall as she gave a rather restrained smile.

"Good evening, Mrs Kane," Rollison greeted formally.

"It is very good of you to see me as late as this," said Mrs Kane.

"It's early for a summer night," protested Rollison politely, and moved round to push a chair into position. Cigarettes in an Arab carved box were on the desk, with a lighter; he opened the box. "Will you smoke?"

"I don't, thank you."

"Then can I get you a drink?"

She hesitated, and Rollison crossed to the cocktail cabinet which stood by the wall near his chair and the table with whisky, a syphon and a glass on it, and went on: "I can offer almost anything."

"Perhaps—gin and bitter lemon, if that's not too difficult."

"The simplest thing in the world," Rollison assured her, and poured the drink and mixed himself a modest whisky and soda. He did not appear to be watching his

A*

visitor closely, but he was. The hangman's rope had caught her eye; it was always the one to attract most attention, and now she was torn between studying him, as if wanting to find out what was in his mind, and in staring at the exhibits on the wall. That was not surprising; among them was practically every kind of weapon which one man could use lethally upon another. From two knives, a small glass case containing some phials of poisons, and a nylon stocking daubed with nail varnish, her gaze travelled to the rope again and then back at Rollison as he advanced with her drink.

"Thank you."

"Cheers," said Rollison, and glanced at the wall. "Terrifying, isn't it?"

"I can imagine that it could be," said Mrs Kane. "I was reading about it this afternoon, in the *Tatler*."

"Oh," said Rollison, and smiled more broadly. "Remember that only half of what you see is true, and practically nothing that you read in any kind of newspaper."

"I didn't expect you to be cynical."

"Not even about newspapers?"

She smiled more freely. "No." She hesitated, and Rollison did not think that she would take long to broach the reason for her visit; she was the type who would go straight to the heart of a subject. Her gaze was very direct and her appraisal obviously thorough. It was impossible to judge whether she approved of tall men whom teenagers insisted on calling handsome and distinguished, or men with nearly black hair flecked slightly with grey, and curling a little, naturally. Rollison knew that in appearance he belonged to a kind of Hollywood world, just as his Trophy Wall belonged to the theatre of olden day melodrama that to some people seemed to make him larger than life, and so it prejudiced them.

He hoped that Mrs Kane would not be prejudiced against him.

He moved round and sat on a corner of his desk. The room was large enough for him to do this without getting too close, and so towering over her; yet it gave him the slight advantage he wanted over anyone who was sitting. He put his glass down, his drink scarcely touched. He was appraising her as openly now, as she was him; in a way, they were fencing.

And after all, he had to break the ice.

"How can I help you?" he asked quietly.

"I would like you to look for my husband," she answered, as quietly.

He wondered what thoughts and fears her eyes were hiding; why she was grave rather than distressed. He wondered what her husband was like, and glanced at her hands and saw the beautiful eternity ring with countless tiny diamonds, evidence of money and surely evidence of love, or at least devotion. She had long, slender hands, slightly brown; her face was slightly tanned, too; she had probably been away during the early summer to some land where sun came less fitfully than to England.

"What makes you think that he is missing?" asked Rollison.

"He has been gone for a week," she answered, "and I've had no message."

"Have you any idea where he's gone?"

"None," said Mrs Kane. "But some of my friends might think they do."

Rollison wanted to ask 'girl friend?' lightly, and so keep tension at bay. He was slightly disappointed, because it looked as if he would have to refuse to help her; looking for erring husbands was not exactly his *métier*. He found himself saying rather stiltedly: "Another woman?"

"Yes," she answered, without hesitation.

"I'm sorry."

"Mr Rollison," said Mrs Kane, quietly, "I am not convinced that my husband has gone away simply because of an attachment, with any girl or woman. He has too much to lose. Reputation, friends and, almost certainly, a considerable sum of money. You won't mind if I am embarrassingly frank?"

Rollison spoke as he stood up. "I ought to be embarrassingly frank first, Mrs Kane. I would much prefer it if you didn't go into distressing domestic details without feeling sure that I shall be able to help." He was a little further away from her, smiling a polite smile, wishing that it was not necessary to talk like this. "Before I could possibly try, I should have to be sure that some crime had been committed, or might be committed, and that there were good reasons why the police couldn't handle the situation. I am"—he spread his hands a little—"what is politely called an amateur criminologist. The things which interest me and claim my time are the causes and the effects of crime. Has one been committed?"

She didn't answer; but her reaction was not quite what he had expected. She would not take 'no' without a struggle, of course, but generally the determination to fight for his help showed in a glint in the eyes, in an expression, somehow even a bodily tension.

At last, she said: "I don't know."

"Do you think—" Rollison began.

"Let me tell you briefly why I have come to you," said Mrs Kane. She sat, relaxed, one hand resting on the desk, the other in her lap; the handbag and umbrella were on the desk. "My husband is a very attractive man, and he finds young women not only attracted to him, but, well—I think 'fascinated' is the word. I have been aware of that for a long time. In marriage, one has to learn to live with the truth, and accept the fact that life is very seldom romantic." The bitterness in the words could not be entirely hidden. "However, he has always kept up appearances. So have I. I cannot believe that he would go off with a girl without making some excuse, or giving some explanation. His business—he is an advertising consultant—often takes him abroad, and to different parts of this country; so there is no great problem of evasion. This time, he simply said that he would be in London for the week-end—last week-end. We live, you see, in Hampshire. He said that he expected to be home by Monday evening." She shrugged, slightly. "I am sure that I ought to look for him."

"Have you been to the police?"

"In these circumstances, would you go to them?" When Rollison didn't answer, Mrs Kane went on: "I understand that the police would only help if they had reason to believe that my husband was officially missing, and I've no more to tell them than I've told you."

"Are you afraid that the police would lead to publicity?"

After a pause, she answered: "Yes."

"Publicity could have a salutary effect on your husband," Rollison said dryly.

"I don't think it would in this case, but I am not concerned for the effect that it would have on my husband," Mrs Kane declared. "It would have a disturbing, perhaps a disrupting effect on my—on our daughter." When Rollison didn't comment, she went on, and actually found it possible to smile. "I told you that my husband was attractive to young girls. My daughter idolises him." When Rollison still did not answer, she went on without any hint of a smile, even with the first touch of tension: "I may be wrong, this may be an *affaire* which has become too strong for him. If it is only that, at least I want to know. I would take no action," she added, as if she knew her own mind exactly. "I am not asking you to look for evidence for a divorce. I won't pretend that I can show any evidence that there is anything unusually wrong—or criminal; all I can say is that this is not normal. It's the middle of July now. My daughter will be home from school in ten days' time, and I need to have some kind of explanation for her. It may seem a very simple domestic problem to you, Mr Rollison, but I can only assure you that it is one of extreme importance to me and my child.

I know of no one else who might help me. Will you, please?"

Perhaps her pride gave her restraint: perhaps she realised that only by that simple, almost dispassionate appeal, could she hope to influence him. There was in fact no reason why he should refuse—and none, except this woman's need, why he should agree. He must make the decision quickly: it would be cruel to keep her waiting.

"Yes," he said.

For the first time, a glimmer of tears showed at her eyes, and it was some time before she said, huskily: "Thank you very much." And then, to help her through that surge of emotion, Rollison asked if she had photographs of her husband and her daughter, and soon looked at a family group, while Mrs Kane said, still huskily: "That is Ralph—and there is Caroline."

Ralph Kane was rather older than Rollison had expected; and Caroline, smiling from a colour tinted photograph with such carefree beauty, made him glad that he had said 'yes'. The immediate problem was to decide how to begin.

2

THE SECOND DISAPPEARANCE

"CAROLINE!" the house-matron called.

Caroline Kane jumped up from her chair in a corner of the tiny, hopelessly untidy study.

"I'm just going to the dorm, matron," she said.

"I didn't come about that, it's barely half-past nine," the matron said. "Miss Abbott wants you."

Caroline exclaimed: "Oh, lor'!" with such crestfallen vehemence that the matron laughed.

"I don't think you've done anything very terrible," she said. "But hurry along. You'd better go straight up to the dormitory afterwards. I'll put your light out."

"Thank you very much," Caroline said.

She hurried along the narrow passage, lit dimly with small-powered lamps, past a dozen study doors, most of them closed and dark, one here and there with a light on and one of the senior girls reading or working, possibly two or three gossiping. At Hapley, a girl was senior at sixteen. Caroline reached the stone landing, out of the matron's sight, and immediately put her hands on the shiny rail at either side of the narrow, stone staircase, lifted her feet, and slid down; she reached the foot with a sharp click of toes and heels, straightened up and turned into a wider passage which had polished linoleum on the floor, and walked sedately towards Miss Abbott's rooms. Bright light came from the top of a door. Caroline slowed down a little, wondering why the house-mistress could possibly want her as late as this, and whether matron was wrong. Abby had a lot of faults, but she was a fair devil, and it wouldn't be 'fair' to carpet anyone at half-past nine; so she really need not worry. Lightly, thoughts of the

minor misdemeanours which might have counted against
her passed through her mind, but these faded as she tapped
at the door and Miss Abbott called:

"Come in."

Caroline opened the door cautiously, saw the house-
mistress sitting in her arm-chair, with some sewing by her
side, and realised that no one else was in the room; that
was a good sign. She smiled; and she did not yet know
how compelling that smile could be, and how even the
most jaundiced and sceptical member of the staff was
affected by it. She had a quality of naturalness, inherited
from her mother, which made her popular with everyone.
She had other qualities, only just beginning to make themselves apparent, which meant that before long men would
be eyeing her. At sixteen, she was as mature in figure as
many women five years older, and she walked with a long-
legged grace which no one could fail to notice.

"Oh, it's you, Caroline. Come in and shut the door."
Miss Abbott, grey-haired, severe looking, very slightly
faded, and dressed now, as she usually was, in a pale grey
suit, always looked cool. There was no censoriousness in
her voice, nothing to suggest trouble. "A rather unexpected
thing has happened," she went on, "and I want you to
keep it to yourself no matter how tempting it may be to
tell the other girls. May I have your promise, please?"

"Yes, Miss Abbott," Caroline answered; and she did not
realise that the house-mistress felt a warmth of affection
for a child who would undoubtedly keep her word. She
herself was more puzzled than ever.

"Very well. You know that we make it a strict rule that
none of the girls may be out of the school grounds after
half-past nine, in any circumstances, but the Head has
agreed that you are going to be the exception." Abby
seemed to be taking pleasure in being mysterious, and
Caroline fought back her impatience with excitement.
"Your father is passing through Hapley Station on the
train which arrives from London at ten minutes to ten,

and stays for ten minutes. He is very anxious to have a word with you, and I told him that you could be at the platform to talk with him."

Caroline's eyes glowed. "Oh, wiz—" she began, and corrected herself almost unthinkingly: "Wonderful! Thank you ever so much, Miss Abbott."

"That's perfectly all right, provided you keep your promise, and you come straight back," Miss Abbott said. "I shall expect you at a quarter past ten. Tap when you're in."

"Oh, I will!"

"And put a coat on, there's a chillier wind than there was this afternoon," said Miss Abbott.

Five minutes later, raincoat over her arm for it was warmer than Miss Abbott had thought, Caroline hurried across the front garden, then through a side gate and out of the school grounds. There was a certain excitement in being here so late; even on a dull evening although it was still daylight, and should be still quite light when she came back. It was twenty minutes to ten, and she had just time to get to the station. Now and again she broke into a run, she was so anxious not to miss a moment of this unexpected meeting. A little breathless, she hardly believed that she was going to see her father, and did not ask herself why he was travelling by train and not by car, as he usually did. She heard a train whistle, a long way off, as she turned towards the station. She knew that it was coming from London, and was almost certainly the one she was going to meet.

She could go along the road, the long way round, or could take a narrow alley, flanked by the wall of a house on one side, and the wall of the station yard on the other. When the school exodus at holiday times was on, the alley was forbidden and the girls had to traipse round by the road, but nothing had been said tonight, and the short cut saved several minutes. Caroline believed that she could hear the chug-chug-chug of the train, but was not quite sure that she would reach the station first. She needed some coppers for a platform ticket, and fumbled in a small purse in the pocket of her dark blue uniform dress. At the end of the alley was the station approach, with its cobbled yard, two or three old taxis almost certainly waiting, the grimy brick walls plastered with coloured posters advertising the glories of seaside resorts. She could even see the cobbles, but a car or taxi pulled up at the end of the passage, and a man jumped out. He stood for a moment looking along the alley towards her, and she hoped that he would not come along it; if he did, she would have to squeeze past him, and she hated pressing against men.

A young woman got out of the car and stood beside him. She was rather short, with a big bust and a very small waist; that showed clearly, because in a way she was in silhouette. She stood peering, like the man. Her hair, dropping almost to her shoulders like Diana Dors', was very fair; it seemed to shimmer.

They didn't come down there.

As Caroline drew nearer, she heard the man say in a tone of deep satisfaction:

"That's her."

Caroline thought: 'I've never seen them before.' The train whistled, further off than she had realised, so she had plenty of time; but these two made her feel uneasy, for some reason she could not understand. Why should they have said 'that's her'? She drew almost level with them, and unless they stood aside she would not be able to get out of the alley.

The woman smiled. She had a very pale face, and no lipstick or rouge; it made her look rather like one or two of the senior girls at school who had worn make-up for the week-end, and cleaned it off for the school week.

"Aren't you Caroline Kane?"

"Yes, that's right," said Caroline. The woman did not trouble her, but she did not like the man at all, He was the type against which Miss Abbott had often warned her; short, rather dark, with heavily greased hair, very dark eyes, like black olives, a jacket with very wide shoulders and trousers that were very narrow, so that the big brown shoes at the bottom of them looked absurd. He was staring at her intently.

"He's ever so sorry, but your father couldn't catch the train," the woman said. "He's very anxious to see you, though, because he has to fly to America first thing in the morning. He's sent us to take you to see him."

Disappointment at the first words faded into doubt and surprise. Her father often travelled unexpectedly, and usually the first intimation Caroline had that he was overseas was a postcard from a foreign country, with just a few bright, casual words, which she had grown used to from him; he seemed to be able to say as much in a sentence as some people could say in a long letter. There was another cause for doubt: these were not the kind of people he associated with, not the kind she would have expected him to use as messengers.

"It's an emergency trip," the man put in.

He had an unexpectedly soft voice, and a surprisingly pleasant smile.

"And he won't be back for six months," the girl urged.

That decided Caroline; if this were such an emergency, and if he were going to be away during the school hols, she had to see him. She had vague thoughts that she ought to send a message to the school, and ought to ask how far away her father was. But the man was opening the door of the car and the girl helped her towards it. It did not occur to her that they were very anxious to make sure that she got in.

"Just a minute," she said, and held back. "I must tell Miss Abbott—that's my house-mistress—that I'll be late. I can telephone over there."

"Your father's sent another message to the school," the man reassured her, and gripped her elbow and seemed to thrust her forward; she felt herself climbing into the car almost against her will, although the answer had come pat, and if it were true there was no need to worry.

She sank down on a cushiony seat, and the blonde got in beside her. The man went to the wheel, moving very quickly, as if this were really a matter of urgency. Almost before she had accepted the situation, Caroline was being driven off, through the familiar streets which soon gave way to the wide country roads. A mile or so away there were crossroads where one could turn for London or for the north. She need not ask where her father was, for she would soon be able to tell which way they were going. Now disappointment because of the holidays was uppermost in her mind.

The car swayed as it turned a corner, and she was thrown against the side; the man was driving very fast, but her father often did, and speed did not worry her at all. As she recovered, she felt a sharp prick of pain in her right forearm, making her gasp. She glanced swiftly at the blonde, and saw that she was concealing something in her right hand; something which glistened.

In sudden panic, Caroline cried: "What's that? What did you do to me?"

"Do? I didn't do anything."

"Yes, you did." Caroline raised her arm quickly, and on the sun-browned skin just below the elbow there was a tiny globule of blood. "You pricked me! What was it?"

"Don't be silly," the other said, rather sharply. "I've a pin in my sleeve, that's all." Whatever she was concealing was hidden by the folds of her full dress now. "Sit back and relax."

Caroline sat back, but could not relax. She wiped the blood off, and it smeared a little. She thought that there was a numb sensation around the spot, but told herself that it might be imagination. She pretended to look out of the window, and after a few moments she felt much more drowsy than she had. Suddenly, she darted her hand towards the folds of the blonde's dress, took her by sur-

prise, touched something hard, and pulled out a hypodermic syringe; she recognised it on the instant.

"No!" she cried. "You've injected something into me.
What are you doing to me? What—"

"*Keep her quiet,*" said the driver roughly, and he swung
the wheel again, pressing her against the door so that
she was quite helpless. That awful feeling of drowsiness
was worse than ever; she felt as if she were losing consciousness, and panic swept over her.

"Let me go!" she cried. "Let me go!" She struck at the
blonde, who was thrusting her hands towards her, and
slapped her sharply across the face. The car swung in
the other direction, and for a moment Caroline was
pressed close against the woman, who was helpless. "*Let
me go!*" she screamed, and then snatched at the handle of
the door, heedless of the fact that they were travelling at
great speed. The handle clicked, and the door sagged
open. But before it swung wide, the driver turned round
and struck her violently on the side of the head, while the
blonde recovered and pushed her away, slammed the
door, and said:

"If you don't keep quiet, you'll really get hurt."

Caroline opened her mouth to scream, although
screaming would be useless on these nearly deserted
country roads. She did not scream, but then, with awful
suddenness, she felt unconsciousness sweeping over her,
felt numbness in her limbs, and sank back.

The car hurtled on.

.   .   .   .

Miss Abbott glanced at the clock on the mantelpiece
and thought: 'She's later than I expected,' but did not
let that worry her. It was not yet half-past ten, and although the train was usually punctual on its way from
London to the north, it had been known to be late, even
in the summer. She got up, pushing her sewing to one side,
yawned, went into the little kitchen where she could make

herself a cup of tea, and put on the kettle. Caroline Kane still hadn't returned when she went into the living-room, and for the first time she began to feel a twinge of alarm. At a quarter past ten she put down a half finished cup of tea, and went to the telephone. As she lifted it and began to dial the station, she told herself that there was no need at all to worry; the train was still at the station, of course.

"British Railways," a man said, perkily.

"I'm sorry to worry you, but can you tell me if the nine-fifty train from London is in yet?"

"Been and gone long ago," the perky man said. "Bang on time tonight, it was. That all?"

"No!" exclaimed Miss Abbott, and felt suddenly breathless with the onrush of a kind of panic which was really born out of the fact that Caroline Kane was always so dependable. "I'm sorry, but I wonder if I could speak to someone who was on duty when the train came in."

"I was, lady."

"I wonder—I wonder if you saw one of the College girls go on the platform," Miss Abbott asked, and immediately blamed herself for having put the question: it might start the man talking, might spread gossip through Hapley for no reason at all. The late return and the fact that the train had been punctual had combined to make her behave foolishly.

"No, miss, there wasn't one," the man answered definitely.

"Oh, but one of the girls went to the platform to meet her father!"

"Surprise me if she did," the man replied. "I was standing in for the ticket collector, and saw everyone on the platform and everyone off. There wasn't one of the College girls here at all, miss. Sure she didn't go to the bus station?"

Miss Abbott clutched at this opportunity, and said as if laughing at herself: "Oh, yes, that must be it. Thank

you very much for your trouble," and rang off. For a
moment she stood quite still, a hand on the telephone,
and then she turned away and hurried out of the room,
into the front garden and across the lawn to a smaller
house, where the headmistress and others of the staff lived
quite close to the road. The extensive grounds of Hapley
lay in front of the main school building. These century-
old buildings were massive and grey in the clear, strangely
vivid evening light. There was a warm wind, rustling
the leaves of beech, sycamore and plane tree. Two junior
members of the staff were coming from the sports field,
swinging racquets, and a smooth-haired terrier went
haring across the lawn in front of her. She reached the
smaller house, and hurried to the headmistress's sitting-
room, and went in. Miss Ellerby, younger by ten years, a
rather heavily-built and not very attractive woman, was
watching television; she looked round almost with
annoyance.

"Why must—" she began, and then stopped short, and
went on: "Maude, what is it?"

Miss Abbott told her . . .

.   .   .   .

After her visit to Rollison, Mrs Kane went into the
small Knightsbridge hotel where she had booked for the
night, and was stepping towards the little self-operated
lift when the elderly man at the desk called:

"Oh, Mrs Kane, there's a message for you. Will you
please ring Hapley 97."

"Hapley—" Caroline's mother began, and immediately her thoughts flashed to the school, to the fact that
this could only be about Caroline. Partly because she was
already so worried, she felt a spasm of real alarm. If
Caroline were ill—her thoughts darted to polio; to an
accident; to appendicitis. She hurried to the lift. "Get
the number for me, Jim, will you?" she asked, and
thought she heard the bell ringing in her room when she

reached the door; but it was in an adjoining room. She did not take off her hat but stripped off her gloves and stared at the window and then at the telephone, every thought of Rollison and his effect on her driven away by these tidings of obvious alarm. "Oh, for heaven's sake!" she began, and then the bell rang, and she picked up the receiver.

3

NIGHT JOURNEY

ROLLISON was getting out of his chair to go to bed when his telephone rang, at a minute or two before midnight. He stepped to his desk quickly, not wanting the bell to disturb Jolly, who did not look at all well; unless he was greatly improved in the morning, he must see a doctor. Rollison thought of Eve Kane, but did not expect this to be her; she hadn't been gone much more than half an hour, after she had told him all—well, most—of her unhappy story. Since she had left, he had been thinking more about her than the story; she was a woman who left a deep impression.

"Richard Rollison speaking."

"Mr Rollison—" Eve Kane said, and then paused, as if she had caught her breath. Her voice was quite unmistakable; so was her agitation. "I'm sorry to worry you again, especially so late, but I've just heard that Caroline has—" there was another pause. Then a single word seemed to be wrung out of her: "Disappeared."

She had talked a great deal about Caroline, and Hapley —a very expensive and fashionable school which catered especially for girls whose parents were often out of the country, many of them living abroad; and which also catered for girls from the Continent, here to put polish on to their English, and to learn English customs. Mrs Kane had enthused on how happy Caroline was at this school, how well she was doing, how desperately anxious her mother was to conceal the estrangement from her.

Rollison said: "Tell me exactly what happened," but before he started, changed his mind. "You'd better tell me on the way to the school, that'll save time."

"You'll come?"

"Of course," Rollison said. "I think you'd better get here as soon as you can, and we'll drive down in my car."

"Thank you," Eve Kane said, chokily. "I can't—"

"Don't try," Rollison said. "Just hurry." He put down the receiver, and stood by it for a moment, trying to understand his own emotions; for his heart was beating faster than usual, and that was not because the case was exciting itself, nor because he was really worried about a schoolgirl he had never seen. He glanced at the Trophy Wall, caught a glimpse of his reflection in a small mirror which had once been used by a murderer, now dead, and went towards his bedroom. There was a light under Jolly's door. He opened this, and saw Jolly sitting up in bed, pale, and with dark patches under his eyes. By Jolly's side was a telephone, and undoubtedly he had listened in. "Did you hear that?" Rollison inquired.

"Yes, sir."

"I don't know when I'll be back," Rollison said, "but I want you to get one of Bill Ebbutt's men to stand in for you, and you must see Dr Welling first thing in the morning."

"I will, sir."

"Fine," said Rollison. "Now sit back, and try to sleep."

"The usual overnight case is packed, sir, except for the toilet bag."

"Fine," Rollison said again. "Good night."

"Good night, sir. And good luck."

Rollison stepped into his own room, found the overnight case with slippers, a change of shoes, pyjamas, a clean shirt, everything he might need in an emergency. He went into the bathroom and collected the oddments he wanted, and then went out. There was a dim yellow light on the landing above the stone steps, which cast grey shadows. He hurried down. The house was silent, and when he stepped into Gresham Terrace, that was also silent but better lit, and there were lights at some of the

windows. He turned right, and hurried towards the mews
where he kept his car. As he turned the corner, a policeman approached, recognised him, and spoke as if it were
a happy chance to meet him.

"Hallo, Mr Rollison. Off out?"

"For a ride in the country," Rollison said. "A friend
of mine is ill."

"I'm sorry about that, sir."

"Sure you are," said Rollison. "Good night." He went
on, hurrying, feeling a great sense of urgency. The mews
was in darkness, and he shone a pencil torch on the
sliding doors of his garage, then switched on the light.
A pearl-grey Rolls-Bentley Continental gleamed beneath
it. Little more than five minutes after leaving the flat, he
was parked outside, watching his wing mirror, sure that
Eve Kane would not be long. Soon, a car turned the
corner; a Sunbeam Alpine. It drew up behind the Rolls-
Bentley and Rollison, already getting out, reached it
before the door opened. He opened it and helped Eve
out. The light showed how bright her eyes were, as if they
were aglint with fear. He had met her for the first time
three hours ago, but there was no sense of strangeness;
he pressed her arm, to try to give some reassurance.

"We'll be there in less than two hours," he said, and
took her to his car. "Did you bring a case?"

"No."

"They'll be able to fix you up at the school," he said.
Soon he was sitting beside her, and the engine was turning
and the car sliding towards the end of the street, Piccadilly, and the north-west. "I'll go out Edgware Road way,
and then work across the suburbs," he said. "I know the
road." They swung into Piccadilly smoothly, and in spite
of the urgency kept down to thirty-five miles an hour.
There was little traffic, and only here and there a policeman, but the Circus was ablaze with light which re-
flected on Eve's pale face and put lurid colours into her
eyes. "What time did it happen?"

"Apparently, about ten o'clock," she answered, and told him exactly what the headmistress of the school had told her, so that he knew as many details as she. In a hopeless kind of voice, she went on: "I can hardly believe this of Ralph. I know that may sound absurd, but I can't."

"Why?"

"She idolised him, but—" There was a moment's pause. "Although he was fond of her, I can't believe that he would want to be responsible for her. It doesn't seem to make sense."

"I see," said Rollison.

He was beginning to wonder what kind of shadow was really looming over this woman. She had jumped to the obvious and probably the right conclusion, and yet she rebelled against it because of what she knew of the character of her husband; and from what she had told Rollison, she was remarkably objective about him. On the other hand, she would not want to believe that her husband was going to leave her for another woman, and wanted to have the child with him.

Once they were in the Edgware Road, he put on speed whenever he could. The car made little more than a humming sound, and Eve sat in silence, as if she could not bring herself to talk about the fresh disaster; probably because she felt that she had already said everything that needed saying.

Suddenly Rollison said: "Could Caroline have run away?"

"I don't think it would even enter her head."

"If your husband hasn't taken her with him, have you any idea what might have happened?" He meant: 'Have you any other, deeper cause for fear?'

"No," she answered. "I've been trying to imagine anyone who might want to harm me, or Ralph, or Caroline. I can't think of anyone. Except—"

Rollison did not prompt her.

"There was a girl who—who threatened him."

"Because he'd let her down?"

"Yes."

"How do you know?"

"She telephoned the house two or three times, and I had to talk to Ralph about it."

"What did he say?"

"He—laughed."

"How long ago was this?"

"About six months," Eve said, and added almost wearily: "I thought what a bad start it was to the New Year. Caroline was in Switzerland with a party of school friends. She's crazy about ski-ing."

"Who was the woman?"

"I only know that her name was Leah."

"Leah," echoed Rollison, and told himself that if it ever became necessary to search for this woman, the name was unusual enough for people to remember its owner more easily than a more commonplace name. "Did she threaten you or Caroline?"

"Oh, no."

Rollison asked: "Is there anyone else?"

"No," Eve said firmly. "No, I've never heard that anyone else made trouble at all. Mr Rollison—"

"Eve," Rollison interrupted, "we're going to work very closely together for the next few days, we'll probably see a lot of each other, and we might just as well make it Eve and Richard—or, if you prefer it, Rolly."

After a pause, she said: "Thank you. I'd like that."

"What were you going to say?"

"Supposing Caroline wasn't taken away by my husband, how—how can you set about trying to find her?"

"We would have to go to the police at once."

"At Hapley?"

"Only to start with," Rollison said. "And even if it was your husband who took her, if we're to stop him from getting away with her, we will have to consult the police."

"Won't it be too late?" asked Eve bitterly.

"You mean, they could have left the country by now?"

"Yes."

"Did Caroline have her passport with her?"

"She had it at school," Eve answered. "I shouldn't think she would have had it with her when she went out tonight. She loved to look at the different continental stamps on it." There was a catch in her voice again. "I think I ought to make one thing clear."

"Yes."

"I'll be guided by you. Do whatever you think best."

"That's the way I like to work!" Rollison said, and glanced at her, smiling. "Headache?"

"Yes."

"In the dashboard pocket in front of you you'll find some aspirins, and fitted inside the door pocket a vacuum jug with water in it. If you'll take three aspirins and close your eyes, you'll get some rest."

"Thank you," she said.

Soon they were on the open road, and the car was moving almost without a sound at eighty miles an hour. Now and again a car approached them, headlights dipping, but for the most part the road was empty. They turned into a main road, had a few miles of driving with heavy trucks going both ways, then turned off.

"You certainly know the way," Eve remarked.

"I've lived in London for a long time," Rollison told her.

When he glanced at her again, she was leaning back with her eyes closed. It was good to think that she could relax even a little; better to know that he had managed to affect her like that. He had a strange feeling, almost of contentment. There was no apparent reason for it, but there it was; a kind of warmth, stealing over him. He had felt like this once or twice before, many years ago and he had forgotten it except in the moments of nostalgic remembering. The almost voluptuous feel of the car, the soft sound of Eve Kane's breathing, the gentle touch of her arm against his because she was leaning slightly this way, were all part of the mood.

He kept glancing in the mirror.

Few cars could match this for speed. There was little danger of being followed, but that was a possibility which he could not neglect. His life had been one of fighting crimes of violence; of surviving because he had kept alert when other men, some clever, some brutal, some vicious and many deadly, had nodded for a moment. This might be a simple domestic matter—but Eve's assessment of her husband's character made it possible that much more was involved. If this were the case of the kidnapping of a child, there might be deep and secret motives, and deep and unknown dangers. So he watched the mirror, to make sure that no car followed. Every one he overtook he studied carefully, so as to recognise it again later if he were forced to stop and the other car passed or stopped also. His was the trained mind, disciplined over the years to miss nothing that might later become significant. He had not told Eve, but if this were not simply a case of a father abducting his child, there might be danger for Eve as well as her daughter. If Caroline had been kidnapped from Hapley Station she must have been watched, and the family and school situation studied closely. If that were true of the daughter, it could be true of the mother.

Eve said unexpectedly: "Rolly." She gave it a long 'o', not short, as in Jolly, but as if it were spelt with only one 'l'. "Why should anyone want to kidnap a child?"

Rollison did not answer, and Eve went on:

"They wouldn't do it without a good reason. Why should anyone want to do it?"

"There are only two possibilities," Rollison said, and it did not occur to him to lie or to hedge; she would want to know exactly what he thought, would not want to be shielded from fears or dangers. "The first is that of revenge, as with this Leah. I wouldn't rate it high unless there was much more than you knew about in his association with her. The other is to bring some kind of pressure to bear."

"Do you mean, ransom?"

"Yes."

"I didn't tell you this," Eve said, and paused before declaring: "I am a wealthy woman—very wealthy, by most standards. I don't care what it costs to get Caroline back."

"I don't think we ought to start thinking of that, yet." Rollison said, although in fact it was on the top of his mind. "I think—"

He stopped, and grew tense, and knew that Eve looked at him, startled. He was staring a little way off the road, for the gleam of the great headlights had picked up a reflection from glass, presumably the windows of a car. Then, swiftly, a car swung out of a road just ahead of them, right in the great car's path.

4

WARNING

ROLLISON trod on the brake and the tyres squealed and he and Eve were thrown forward. She banged her head on the windscreen, and he heard her gasp. The car, vivid in the headlights, had turned in the direction that they were going, and seemed to be moving fast. It might be a lunatic of a driver; or it might have been done deliberately, to slow him down and to stop him.

Brake lights went on.

The nose of the Rolls-Bentley and the tail of the leading car were only two yards apart, now, but there was no danger of a heavy collision. The leading car was still slowing down, as if the driver were set on stopping them. Eve was sitting back with a hand at her head, as if she were dazed; too dazed, perhaps, to be frightened.

Rollison swung his wheel, missed the bumper of the car ahead by a fraction of an inch, and roared past it. He saw the gargoyle-like face of the man at the driving seat, looking as if he had a hand on the door, ready to open it, but terrified that it should be smashed out of his grasp. Another face was staring from the far side of the car. Rollison said: "Sorry", and swung the wheel again, so that he was in front and only a few yards ahead of the second car. He stopped, and said:

"Are you all right?"

"Yes, it's made me a bit dizzy, that's all."

"I'll go and see if I can make that driver dizzy," Rollison said grimly.

"No, please don't! It will lose time."

"I won't let it," Rollison assured her, and opened the door and swung out on to the road. There was still a possibility that it was no accident, but a deliberate attempt to stop him. If so, he wanted to see the driver, a quick counter-attack now could save a lot of trouble later on. There was no need for Eve to know that he half-expected danger—it would be bad enough if she had to know about it if it were true. If it were, he was a sitting bird; but he kept close to the side of the road, watching closely. There was no move from the car. When Rollison reached it, the driver was still sitting at the door, but the window was down.

"What the hell are you playing at?" Rollison demanded.

"S-s-sorry," the driver muttered, and he still looked scared. "I thought you were further away."

"You could have killed us as well as yourself."

"Yes, I—I know. I'm sorry."

It was too natural to be acting; this had been just a piece of lunatic driving. The girl next to the driver looked scared, too; and they were both young.

"You might remember that you've got just one life," Rollison said. He felt pompous, and sounded it, partly because of the anti-climax. He realised that in his mind he had almost taken it for granted that the driver had deliberately set out to stop him. "Good night."

He was half-way back to his own car before the response from the couple in the car came. He got in next to Eve, who didn't speak until he had started off again. Then she said:

"Did you think they did that deliberately?"

"I thought it just possible." He put his foot down harder, and the needle spun round to the sixties. "In the kind of crime I'm used to working on, that sort of thing does happen often, and the wise thing is to assume that it was deliberate." He still sounded pompous, and wished that he didn't: he wanted to impress Eve Kane well. "It didn't take a minute, did it?"

"No."

"How's your head?"

"The bump started it aching again, but I'll be all right. How long will it be before we reach the school?"

"About half an hour."

"I'll take your advice again, and close my eyes."

"Do that," said Rollison.

Eve seemed to settle back in the luxurious seat, and he stared at the winding road ahead of him, seeing the glow of lights in the sky from car headlamps. The little encounter had shaken him, because it had shown how easy it would be to do the wrong thing. Usually, he was quite sure of himself. Now, he felt doubts—and he knew that the chief reason for the doubt was anxiety not to fail this woman.

He glanced at her. The faint light from the instrument panel shone on her profile; a very lovely profile. He pictured her as he had seen her when she had first entered his room, tall, easy moving, with those wide-set blue eyes and the outward calmness concealing the depth of her distress. He put his foot down harder, getting all the speed he could. Eve did not stir, and once he wondered if she had dropped off to sleep from sheer mental and emotional exhaustion; but she moved her position slightly, and in a way which told him that she was wide awake. She didn't speak.

Twenty minutes after they had started off again, she sat up.

"That's Old Castle," she said. "It's only a mile or two now. Do you know where the school is?"

"No."

"I'll direct you," she said. "When we get into the town, there's a forked road, and we take the left, past the station."

"Thanks." They reached the fork very soon, and as he turned left, she said: "It's the third on the right. You'll see a church on the left, and the drive to the main buildings and the headmistress's house is just there."

Rollison sensed that she had regained her composure, as completely as she was likely to. Soon the church loomed up, the spire tall and graceful against the stars beyond.

"Now slow down—it's the second on the left. The drive goes straight to the headmistress's house, and you can park just outside it. I expect someone will be waiting for us." Eve was doing something to her hair, Rollison realised, and he smiled faintly, then slowed down when he saw two figures appearing in the headlights, so suddenly that they startled him; then he realised that they were two women in the entrance to the school drive. He slowed down.

"There's Miss Abbott!" Eve exclaimed.

"The house-mistress?"

"Yes."

Miss Abbott looked tall and lean and grey in the light; and she was nearer the car than the other, smaller woman. A man came limping from one side as Rollison stopped, and Eve leaned out of the window.

"Is there any news, Miss Abbott?"

"I'm terribly sorry, but there isn't."

Eve said: "Oh," and seemed to go tense. "Has Miss Ellerby told the police?"

"Not since you specially asked that she shouldn't," Miss Abbott answered, "but she is anxious to, just in case it isn't quite what it seems. She is waiting for you. You drive on, and I'll follow. There's no one else in the car park."

She did not ask who Rollison was, but he noticed that the smaller, dumpier woman who had not spoken was staring at him; so was the man. The gravel of the drive crackled beneath the wheels, and the starlight showed a great stretch of open land, of lawn, and a row of smaller houses and a large building, obviously the main school building. Lights were on at two of the houses, and streamed from the front door of one of them. Rollison pulled up outside this. As he switched off the engine, he heard the footsteps of Miss Abbott and the other woman, and footsteps coming from inside the house, too; a shadow was cast near the car, and rapidly touched and then climbed up it. A massive woman appeared as Rollison helped Eve out: her voice was gruff and mannish.

"Mrs Kane," she said, "I'm dreadfully sorry about this."

"I'm sure you are," Eve responded.

"I know how difficult it must be for you," the massive woman went on, "but I really think that we ought to call the police at once. I am very deeply disturbed."

"May we talk about the police?" asked Rollison. He knew that the woman was scrutinising him closely, and the light fell clear upon his face. There was no hint of recognition; in London he might be recognised by many people, but that was much less likely here.

"Miss Ellerby, this is Mr Rollison, who has kindly promised to help me," Eve introduced; she still held on to her composure. "Rolly, this is Miss Ellerby, the head-mistress."

"*The* Mr Rollison?" asked Miss Ellerby, without a moment's pause. Although her large face was in shadow, it was easy to see that she was very tense. "Dare I use the soubriquet—the Toff?"

Bless her heart!

"That's right," said Rollison lightly.

"By all accounts, you'll be able to help as much as the police," declared Miss Ellerby. She had a very emphatic manner and the gruffly mannish voice was powerful; she might be speaking because of the feeling of tension. "Whatever you think, I must say that I feel it would be a great mistake not to go to the police. I sent Higgs, the porter, to the station to find out what he could, and there was an incident which worries me very much. But please come in. And you, Abby. Mrs Higgs, I'm sure that Mrs

Kane could do with a cup of tea or coffee—which would you prefer, Mrs Kane?"

"Coffee, please."

"Yes, m'm," the dumpy woman said, and went round the back of the house, while Rollison followed the other women into the well-lighted passage, then into a large, square, equally well-lighted room, one wall of which was filled from floor to ceiling with books. There were several very comfortable looking arm-chairs; this looked a man's rather than a woman's room. "Do sit down," Miss Ellerby said. On close inspection she proved to have a hardy-looking outdoor kind of face, and very bright and rather beady blue eyes; her face was too fleshy, and so was her body, but it was firm flesh; there was nothing flabby about her.

"What was this particularly worrying incident?" asked Rollison.

Eve was stripping off her gloves, and showed no sign of wanting to sit down.

"Higgs tells me that there was only one porter on duty at the ticket barrier near the front of the station," answered Miss Ellerby. "And when the London train came in there were only two taxis, and both drivers were waiting with their passengers on the platform—that kind of thing happens at Hapley, Mr Rollison; there is still a great sense of courtesy, and taxi drivers carry luggage. This porter, a young man named Smart, says that he saw a large car, a Humber Super Snipe 1951 model, black, draw up at the entrance to Station Lane, an alley which Caroline would probably take as it is a short cut to the station. He says that two people got out, a man and a woman, and went to the other side of the car, that is the alley side; when they drove off, he saw three people in the car. Apparently a taxi had driven up in the meantime and his attention was distracted for a few minutes, so that he didn't see anything else; but he was quite sure that there was an extra person in the car when it drove off. I *really* think you should inform the police—unless, Mrs Kane, you know what is behind this disturbing situation?"

"I don't know anything about it. I'm only frightened of what it may be."

"Forgive me for being frank, but is there an estrangement between you and your husband?"

"Yes."

Miss Ellerby said: "Oh dear, oh dear." She glanced at Miss Abbott, who was in the doorway. "And you don't want scandal?"

Rollison answered: "We just want to find Caroline. May I use your telephone?"

"Of course."

"Thank you," Rollison said, and smiled at Eve, trying to give her some reassurance. "I think we can start a search for that car without giving anything else away yet." He saw the hope which sprang into her eyes, and the new evidence of tension in Miss Ellerby, who had such a responsibility for the missing girl. Along the passage there was a rattle of cups. He dialled O, and Miss Ellerby said: "If it's a long distance call, just give this number and then the one you want."

"Thanks ... Whitehall 1212, please," Rollison said into the telephone, then covered the mouthpiece with his hand, and said to the others: "The man in charge there tonight is an old friend of mine; he'll help. Don't be surprised if you don't quite recognise the story I'm going to tell him." He saw Mrs Higgs come in, carrying a tray laden with cups, saucers and sandwiches, and Miss Abbott followed with the coffee. The Yard answered. "Superintendent Marshall, please," Rollison said, and a moment later heard a man's deep voice. "Nick ... Rollison here."

He chuckled when the other man said: "I didn't think it would be long before you got restless again. What do you want?"

"Nick, some friends of mine have lost some valuables, and they think they were taken off in a Humber Super Snipe . . ." Rollison gave all the details, and then went on quite easily: "The car was seen at about ten o'clock at Hapley Station, and no one knows whether it was heading north or south. How well do you know the Hapley chaps? . . . Or the county coppers? . . . Yes, if you would, it would be a great help. What? . . . Oh, furs mostly, but it's the car I'm after." He chuckled. "Thanks, I know you will . . . Leave a message for me at Hapley 97, will you?"

He rang off.

Miss Ellerby said: "It's nice to know you act as quickly as your reputation. I feel easier in my mind already." She didn't look it. "Do sit down, Mrs Kane. Black or white coffee, Mr Rollison?" Miss Ellerby was doing her best to make sure that the whole proceedings were kept on a matter-of-fact level, and she had everything very well organised, for Mrs Higgs had gone and Miss Abbott, who had a surprisingly friendly but horse-like face, was pouring out the coffee. "I must congratulate you on one thing, Mrs Kane. I am quite sure that Caroline did not even suspect that there was any trouble at home. There are times, you know, when it is better for a child to be warned. Children are much tougher and hardier creatures than parents think. Their minds are most resilient and their emotions, too. I don't have a lot of time for some of the methods of advanced psychiatrists, you know; my experience with girls over a period of nearly thirty years is that they are born with most of the qualities they reveal, good or bad, and that only a child born with a peculiarly sensitive and abnormal metabolism really suffers any permanent scar from parental problems." Whether she really believed that or not, she made it sound as if she did. "Do you think that Mr Kane has abducted Caroline?"

Eve did not answer.

Miss Abbott dropped a spoon.

There were footsteps in the passage, the bustling ones of Mrs Higgs, and perhaps they stopped Eve from answering. Mrs Higgs appeared and stood foursquare in the doorway, carrying an envelope which was badly crumpled. Rollison had an impression that there was a kind of constant cold war between her and Miss Ellerby.

"What is it?" Miss Ellerby asked sharply.

"I just saw this in the letter basket. I don't know how long it's been there," said Mrs Higgs with a kind of aggressive defensiveness, as if she expected to be blamed for not having found it earlier. "I thought you would like it at once, Miss Ellerby."

"Yes. Thank you," Miss Ellerby said. "Give it to Miss Abbott." Mrs Higgs obeyed, and went off, a dumpy and heavy-footed woman, burdened up with some kind of grievance or disapproval. Miss Abbott took the letter and crossed the room with it.

"It's addressed to the headmistress," she remarked as she glanced at the envelope, and handed it over. "I wonder when it was delivered." Rollison saw the new tension on Eve's face, the eager interest of Miss Abbott's, and the forced composure of Miss Ellerby's as she opened the envelope. It was obviously too late to try to trace whoever had delivered it.

She drew out a lock of silky, auburn-coloured hair, tied round with a piece of string from which was dangling a crumpled card. There was a moment of shocked silence before Eve cried:

"That's Caroline's!" She half ran across the room and snatched it from the headmistress's grasp. "It *is* Caroline's. Oh, dear God, what has happened to her?" She held the lock of wavy auburn hair in one hand and poised the fingers of the other over the card, as if she were afraid.

Rollison said urgently: "Don't touch it, please," and reached her side in two strides, held the card gingerly by one tip, and then took the other corner, so that the words written on it in block letters were easy to read. Miss Ellerby and Miss Abbott had moved round so that they could see it, too.

It read: *"Don't go to the police or you won't see her again."*

5

GUILTY FATHER?

ROLLISON felt Eve trembling; this was almost more than she could stand. Still holding the card by one corner, he put his free arm round Eve's shoulders, and led her towards one of the large arm-chairs. Miss Abbott patted a cushion. Eve lowered herself into the chair and sat for a few moments, staring blankly in front of her; only the twist of her lips and the way her eyes were narrowed told of her anguish.

"I'd like to cut this string," Rollison said. "There might be fingerprints on the card." He wasn't surprised that Miss Ellerby went straight to a small Welsh dresser of dark oak, and picked up a pair of scissors. "And can I have two clean envelopes? We need to keep the envelope that this came in." Miss Abbott and Miss Ellerby fetched envelopes and waited on him, until the card and the crumpled envelope were quite safe. Throughout all this, Eve had sat staring in front of her, but as Rollison pushed the protected card and envelope into his pocket, she said explosively:

"I can't believe that it's Ralph."

"It would surely have been signed, if it were from him," Miss Ellerby declared, and looked at Rollison.

"I can't believe that he would have allowed other people to come and take Caroline away," said Eve. "I'm *quite* sure that he wouldn't do anything as crude as this."

"Then why—" Miss Abbott began, but stopped at a sign from the Head.

"The obvious possibility is that she will be held to ransom," Rollison said, and wasn't surprised to see the

43

shocked reaction on Miss Abbott's horsey face. "But there's nothing to indicate that yet."

"Mr Rollison," Miss Ellerby said in much the tone of voice she used when talking to Mrs Higgs.

"Yes?"

"How thoroughly will the police look for the car? Are you sure that it wouldn't be better, in the circumstances, to tell them what this is about? They will surely treat the matter with a greater sense of urgency."

"They won't slack," Rollison assured her.

"The official you spoke to might have thought that your interest was very casual."

"He would take it for granted that it was urgent if not desperate, or I wouldn't have asked for help," retorted Rollison. "You can be quite sure that the local police are already making inquiries about that car. It won't be easy to find out much about it until the morning, but you can be sure that police patrols and beat-duty police-men in the towns and cities within a hundred miles will have been alerted. I'd like to talk to that porter, Smart," he added, and his sense of urgency showed in his manner.

"He didn't see the number of the car. Higgs asked him," announced Miss Ellerby.

"You'd be surprised how much people see without realising it until they're questioned," Rollison said drily. "Do you know his address?"

"He'll still be at the station, he's on night duty."

"I'll go and find him," Rollison decided. "Meanwhile, I'd like all three of you to exercise your own memories to see if you know anything that might help, but which you've forgotten." He was looking intently at Eve. "Eve, this is especially important for you. Have you had the slightest indication that anything like this might happen —indications that you wouldn't appreciate before the event, but which might drop into perspective now that it's happened?"

"What kind of thing?" demanded Miss Ellerby.

"Has Caroline been watched? Has she had anything to do with anyone in Hapley, outside the school? Has anyone shown any special interest in Caroline or in you, Eve? Has anyone asked for or expected money from you that they haven't received? Has any friend of yours a Super Snipe of this colour and year? Has Ralph shown any sign that he would like possession of Caroline? Has—"

"I've told you that, he hasn't."

"Think harder," urged Rollison. "Has he said or done anything lately to suggest that he might take some kind of violent or unexpected step? Have you had any special quarrel lately? If he has been screwing himself up to do this, he might have acted out of character by employing other people; we can't rule that out. Ask each other questions, to be as searching as you can."

"We will, indeed," Miss Ellerby assured him, with a grim note in her voice.

Rollison finished his coffee and went out, finding that there was a spit of rain in the air as he reached the car. He had plenty of room to turn round, and drove back the way he had come, remembering a sign pointing to the station. Now he saw a finger-post pointing at what seemed a blank wall; that was probably Station Alley. He pulled up just past it, took out his pencil torch, stepped into the unlit alley and shone the torch towards the cobbles. Almost at once he saw a sixpence, leaning between two cobblestones, and picked it up. At the far end of the alley there was a glow of light, and he thought he heard voices, but he could not be sure. There were no footsteps. He shone the beam from side to side, wishing that it were brighter, wishing still more that it was daylight. He found a screwed-up cigarette packet, the shaggy ends of several cigarettes, a crushed ice-cream carton and several spent matches. Then he reached the end of the alley, and two men loomed up, big and threatening.

So there had been voices.

"Would you mind telling me what you are doing, sir?" one of them asked.

"The same as you, I think," Rollison said. "Looking for two people who were here in a Humber Snipe earlier this evening."

"How did you know about that, sir?"

"I asked the Yard to look out for it," answered Rollison. "Have you chaps spoken to the porter, Smart?"

The man on the right said: "Yes. He saw the car. May I have your name and address, sir?"

"Richard Rollison, of 22 Gresham Terrace, Mayfair," answered Rollison promptly, and took a card out of his pocket with a movement that was almost sleight of hand. "Are you C.I.D. or uniformed branch?"

"C.I.D., sir."

The other man was looking at the card in the poor light.

"Turn that over," Rollison said, "and—"

The man obeyed, and saw a little sign on the other side: a top hat, a monocle, a cigarette in a holder, and a bow tie; a man, in fact, without a face. Immediately the officer flashed a look at him, his manner changed subtly, and there was a touch of eagerness in his voice:

"It's Mr Rollison, Jeff—the Toff."

"Good God!" gasped the C.I.D. man.

Rollison said: "What I'd very much like is to have a word with Smart, on my own, and you to take this along to your headquarters and have the contents tested for fingerprints." He handed over the envelope in which the lock of hair had come, but kept the card. "I don't really know what this is all about yet, but I'll come over to headquarters as soon as I've finished with Smart. What's he like, by the way? Reliable?"

"He's a bit too cocky, otherwise he's all right," the officer told him. "Do you know how to get to our place, sir?"

"No."

"Jeff, you bring Mr Rollison along, I'll go and get this

fixed." The spokesman was obviously determined to show that what the Yard could do, Hapley could do as well if not better. "See you later, sir."

"Fine," said Rollison. "Er—just one thing."

"Yes, sir?"

"Except for your chief, don't tell anyone I'm here, will you?"

"Mum's the word, sir!"

The man went off, and Jeff stood by Rollison, who said: "Come and introduce me to this man Smart, will you?" and they crossed the uneven cobbled yard. The C.I.D. man got into a car and the engine roared. A small figure loomed out of the gloom of the station booking-office, and Rollison saw a perky man, peaked hat on one side, who seemed to be wearing a uniform a little too large for him.

"I'm a friend of one of the mistresses at the girls' school," Rollison said.

"Oh, Miss Ellerby's."

"That's right. I—"

"Told the school porter all I know when he rang up to find out if I'd noticed anything. Can't do more than that," Smart said, as if he were tired of the whole business.

"Did you see these two people from the Snipe?"

"Course I saw them."

"What were they like?"

"The man was a proper Teddy boy type but a bit older, that's all," Smart answered. "And the girl— phew!" He made exaggerated curvaceous shapes in the air. "More like an egg-timer, she was; haven't seen one with a bigger pair for a long time! Couldn't mistake her. Hasn't this kid turned up?"

"She will," Rollison said. He knew that the C.I.D. man was within earshot, and must be wondering about the talk of a 'kid'. "What else did you notice about the girl?"

"She was a blonde, like I told Miss Abbott on the phone. If you ask me, I did pretty well. Only had a look now and again. I had passengers to look after and a dozen things to do at once. Haven't got eyes out of the back of my head, have I? I—" He broke off startled, when Rollison held out his hand, and a pound note was neatly transferred; the feel and the rustle of paper created a great change in the manner of Smart the porter. "Always do the best I can, especially for anyone up at the girls' school."

Two minutes later, walking along the alley to his car, Rollison said to Jeff:

"The father of one of the girls at the College seems to have wanted to get care of his daughter before the marriage broke up. That's why we want to keep this as quiet as we can." The story would serve for the Hapley police for a while, at least. At the back of Rollison's mind was the thought of that curt message on the card still in his pocket: the card which was more likely to have fingerprints than the envelope.

"*This* yours, sir?" said Jeff, as they reached the Rolls-Bentley. "What a beauty! After you, sir."

He stood back, holding open Rollison's door; and Rollison saw two things at the same moment. On his seat was something small and white, like a visiting card; and not far along the road a small car was parked, without lights, so that he could not read the registration number. He did not think Jeff saw the white thing. He got in, touching the card, which seemed about the same size as the one which had been delivered to Miss Ellerby. He switched on the reading light, and glanced down. It said: "*Get £20,000 ready, in cash. They must be old notes.*"

Well, that didn't surprise him, and was not desperately urgent. He slid it into his pocket, and a moment later, eased off the brake and began to move along. The parked car didn't move. He purred past, glancing towards it as Jeff said:

"Our chaps will get him all right; crazy place to park without lights. Not so bad under a lamp." He seemed to take no more interest in the little car, but Rollison saw its side lights go on, and realised that they were drawing nearer as he went slowly towards the main part of the town. The car number still did not show up.

On his own, he would have known exactly what to do; with the C.I.D. man beside him, it was difficult to decide. He turned a corner under Jeff's direction, and a minute later the small car turned too. If the driver was deliberately following him, and that seemed likely, he would soon know about the visit to the police station. The warning on the card might be serious: it would be taking too great a risk to ignore it.

"Jeff," he said, "there's just a chance that there'll be a message at Miss Ellerby's. Mind if I look in there first?"

Jeff said promptly: "Of course not," and gave him directions.

The little car followed.

The problem now was to get hold of the driver while shaking Jeff off, and it was not going to be easy.

"I don't know whether you know it, Mr Rollison," Jeff said suddenly, in a conspiratorial undertone, "but a Hillman's been on our tail for the last few minutes. Why don't you stop suddenly in the middle of the road, and let me jump out and tackle the blighter?"

6

JEFF

So Jeff was smart.

If he were so quick on the uptake, he would quickly guess if Rollison tried to fool him. The only wise thing was to let him do what he suggested. The police could be as discreet as anyone, and if they believed that Caroline Kane was in danger, they would certainly be discreet over this; more harm would come from trying to pull the wool over Jeff's eyes than in giving him his head.

"Right," whispered Rollison, and then realised that there was no need to keep his voice down. "I'll pull in towards the school drive. He won't be surprised to see the rear light go on then." The drive showed up dimly beneath a street lamp, twenty or thirty yards away. The car hardly moved, and when it stopped it was with the gentlest of a forward sway.

Jeff's left hand was already on the door handle, and he pressed down and flung open the door almost before the car had stopped. He was swivelling round, legs thrust towards the open door, too, and in a flash he was standing alongside the car, then racing back towards the little car, which was fifty or sixty yards behind him. Rollison, saw him vaguely in the mirror, which was anti-glare and, by night, filled with shadows. He saw the headlights of the car go on. One moment Jeff was a shadowy figure, the next he showed up stark and vivid and black, arms still stretched out as if defying the driver of the small car to try to pass on either side. Rollison pushed open his door and started to get out. The headlights went off for a second, and then shone out again. Rollison's feet were on the ground and he was starting towards Jeff and the small car, when, horrified, he realised what the driver intended to do.

"*Look out, Jeff!*" Rollison bellowed.

Jeff would know what was coming as well as he did; he was moving forward, obviously at a disadvantage, and unable to fling himself to one side in the split second that he had left. The small car's engine roared. "*Look out!*" Rollison shouted again, but it was useless, there was nothing he could do.

Jeff leapt desperately towards the right.

He showed up vividly in the headlights, but the driver of the car was just a shape.

Rollison felt as if the car were coming at him. He stood quite still and held his breath. He saw Jeff fall. He saw the car strike him, and lurch over him. He heard a choking cry. He saw Jeff's arms rise for a moment, and then flop down. By then, the small car was coming at Rollison as if determined to mow him down, also. Rollison flung himself to one side, and on to the boot of the Bentley. The car swept by, engine still roaring, and he felt the wind of its passing. He scrambled off the back of the big car. The rear light of the other seemed a long way off, and suddenly the headlights swivelled, as it turned a corner to the left; and then the rear lights vanished, and the street seemed very dark.

There was no sound from Jeff.

Rollison felt a fierce urge to rush into the driving seat and hunt the car down, but he forced himself to swing round, and run towards Jeff. Only the distant hum of the vanished car's engine sounded. "*Higgs!*" he shouted at the top of his voice. "*Higgs!*" A light at the window seemed to mock him; so did the small lamp near the entrance to the school, only a few yards away. "*Higgs!*" he bellowed, and then reached Jeff's side. There was sufficient light for him to see how motionless the detective was. Jeff's face was turned away from him, and he lay on his stomach. Rollison called out for the porter again, his voice pitched high, then shone his tiny torch with its pitifully slender beam. It shone on the crimson of blood, and on Jeff's hand; it shone on a dark stain on Jeff's white shirt, where the coat had been caught up; and it shone on the tyre marks across the shirt and the top of the trousers, the car must have gone right over him.

The murderous swine . . .

A man came, hurrying, not far along. "*Help!*" Rollison called, and saw a uniformed policeman passing beneath a street lamp. At the same time, Higgs limped from the driveway; so the shouting had not been useless. "Ambulance, quickly," Rollison called. "A man's been run over." He saw Higgs hesitate, and then the policeman drew up, gasping for breath but managing to ask:

"Is he hurt badly?"

"Very."

The policeman did a simple thing: he blew his whistle.

.   .   .   .

Now Rollison had to decide how much to tell the men at the police station as well as how much to tell Eve. He could imagine what she would feel if she believed that her daughter had been taken away by people who would act as ruthlessly and cruelly as the driver of the small car. He was still suffering from a kind of shock, and had not really started to ask himself why the driver had been so ruthless and cold-blooded.

Jeff was already on his way to the hospital. The constable had asked the formal questions and Rollison given the formal answers. Miss Ellerby had come out to see what the fuss was about, had been told there had been an 'accident' and had gone back, with that tight-lipped tension. Rollison had not seen Eve again yet. A car drew up and the policeman he had seen at the railway station got out, with a tall, thin man whose hair showed very silvery in the lamp light.

"Mr. Rollison, this is Chief Inspector Dawson," he introduced.

"Glad to know you, Mr Rollison." Dawson had a slow speaking voice. "Not going to try to persuade me that this was a coincidence, are you?"

That made Rollison's mind up for him.

"No," he said. "Will you come into Miss Ellerby's house, and give me a few minutes with the mother of a girl who's missing? Then I'll tell you what I know."

"Very well," Dawson said. He made that sound ominous.

Eve was with Miss Abbott and Miss Ellerby in the big room. Her eyes seemed frightened, and she looked at him as if she had some premonition that the news he brought would not be good. The two mistresses went out, and Eve stepped towards Rollison, and said in a taut voice:

"She isn't hurt, is she?"

"I still haven't the faintest idea where she is," Rollison told her. "But we're going to have to tell the police some of the truth, in spite of that note."

Eve didn't speak.

"I don't think your husband is responsible," Rollison went on. "I can't believe that this has anything to do with your married life, either."

Eve caught her breath. "Why?"

"A policeman has been run down and badly injured, trying to talk to one of the men we think are concerned," Rollison said, hating the need to give greater cause for fear. "The driver of the car got away. He may not have intended murder, but it was a murderous assault." He was watching her all the time, sharing her distress, admiring how she fought against breaking down. "I'll have to tell the police and ask them to keep it from the newspapers. I think they will, so I don't think the people who have taken Caroline need know that the authorities have been told, but there's no certainty."

"I see," Eve said stonily. "You must do what you think best."

"Have you thought of anything that might explain what has happened?"

"Only—ransom."

"Have you the slightest idea who might be behind it?"

"No," Eve said. "No idea at all."

"Would they be likely to try to get ransom from your husband as well?"

"No."

"Why not?"

"He isn't rich," she answered, and her eyes closed for a moment; Rollison thought that she would faint. "He has a good income, that's all."

"Is he a private consultant?"

"No," she told him. "He's a consultant with Colfax World Advertising. He travels for them, he—" She broke off. "Are you—are you sure that talking to the police wouldn't make things worse for Caroline?"

"Eve," Rollison said, "we can't be positive about anything, except that the police will help all they can. You needn't be present when I tell them."

"I'd rather know everything that's going on," she said.

Dawson, the policeman whose name was Moss, and the three women were all back in the big, square room while the whole story was related. Once he knew that he was being told everything, Dawson became prosily co-operative, and there must have been some measure of reassurance for Eve in his words. A widespread search was already on for the Super Snipe as a result of the Yard's request. He, Dawson, had been in touch with the police of all the neighbouring counties. Rollison's description of the Hillman which had run Jeff down had already been telegraphed to all nearby police stations, and all small cars on the road would be searched and all Hillmans examined.

"We can deal with this simply as a hunt for a man who

ran down one of our men," explained Dawson carefully. "It need not be connected with your daughter's disappearance, yet, Mrs Kane. Except in case of dire emergency, it never will be." He seemed a little ill-at-ease when he looked across at her. "Mr Rollison, I've had that envelope tested for prints, and there are only three sets— Miss Ellerby's, Mrs Higgs's and Miss Abbott's. The address must have been written by someone wearing gloves. From what I've seen of this card, the same can be said of that."

"You mean they don't help?" Eve asked.

"We cannot assume that by a long way," Dawson said didactically. "There are a dozen ways that it can be of assistance, and—" He paused momentarily, for the telephone bell rang, an unexpected thing so late at night. Miss Ellerby stepped across and lifted the receiver with obvious impatience.

"Miss Ellerby speaking ... Yes, he is," she said at once, and looked at Rollison. "It's a London call, Mr Rollison, for you."

That could only be the Yard.

"Thanks," Rollison said, and took the receiver while everyone in the room stared expectantly. "Rollison speaking ... Oh, yes, Nick?"

Superintendent Marshall said sharply: "Is your inquiry about a Super Snipe connected with the running down of that policeman at Hapley?"

"Yes."

"Then I want to know exactly what's on." Marshall was even sharper.

"The local police will brief you. I told them directly their man was run down," Rollison assured him. "Keep it right away from the Press, Nick, until I see you."

"Sure I should?"

"I think you'll be making a grave mistake if you don't," Rollison answered carefully. "Have you found any trace of the car?"

"I think so."

Rollison asked: "What, exactly?" and tried not to show by the inflection in his voice that there was news of any kind, since nothing in Marshall's manner suggested that it was good.

"It was one of the staff cars belonging to the Colfax Advertising Agency," Marshall told him. "It was taken out eight days ago by a Captain Ralph Kane, an advertising consultant of the Colfax. Kane hasn't kept any appointments since. I don't know much about it because very few of the Colfax people can be found at this hour, but I did get the company's secretary out of bed. The car was found parked inside London Airport, and arrived about the time you'd expect if it was driven from Hapley. No others did, and there's a copy of a Worcester newspaper in it, so it came from there. I've got the airport police trying to trace whoever was in it, and where they went. There was one thing found in the car which I don't like the sound of."

"What?"

"The broken needle of a hypodermic syringe," Marshall said. "It's being tested to see if we can find out what it was used for, and whether it was used recently. Is this a kidnapping or an abduction case?"

7

SECOND NOTE

"So it is Ralph," Eve said in a flat voice.

"It begins to look as if your husband is involved," agreed Dawson. "There is at least one great reassurance in that, Mrs Kane."

"I can't think of one."

"In your husband's care, your daughter is not likely to come to any harm. The use of the hypodermic syringe suggests that she was put to sleep quickly, probably in order to avoid frightening her more than necessary."

"I suppose so."

"You can be absolutely sure that everything possible will be done," Dawson assured Eve earnestly. "Apart from your daughter, we want to get the man who ran Jeff down, and we do not intend to lose any time. The Yard will feel just as strongly, and the best available men will be working on this case until we've solved it."

"Thank you," Eve said woodenly.

Rollison, watching first one and then another, saw how unimpressed Eve was, and how impatient Miss Ellerby was getting. Miss Abbott looked ghostly pale, and her eyes were large and glassy; she was not used to being up in the early hours of the morning. Dawson, with his grim earnestness, also had an impatient look as he went on:

"I'm sure that Mr Rollison will co-operate in every way, and you have my absolute assurance that nothing will be done that is not in the interests of your daughter."

"Thank you," Eve said mechanically.

"I think it's time we all had some rest," Miss Ellerby interpolated, energetically. "It won't do any good if we stay up all night. Is there anything more we can do for you, Mr Dawson?"

"I would like to look through the young pupil's desk and belongings," answered Dawson. "There is a possibility that we shall find some indication there—"

"Oh, nonsense," Miss Ellerby exclaimed.

"It is essential not to leave any stone unturned," insisted Dawson, and Miss Ellerby threw up her arms and looked almost furiously at Miss Abbott. "Miss Abbott, I'm sorry it's so late, but will you please take Mr Dawson wherever he wants to go? Try not to wake the girls, won't you? If they get any idea of the gravity of this situation they'll talk about nothing else tomorrow." She was still brisk, still held herself under rigid self-control. "Mrs Kane, I think you ought to go to bed with a hot drink and a sedative. My spare room—"

"Rolly, are we going to help at all by staying here?" Eve asked, and Rollison, noticing how easily and naturally she used the 'Rolly', had a moment of real satisfaction.

"I don't see how we could help," he answered.

"Have you enough energy to drive me back to London?"

"Of course."

"I think it is ridiculous to return," declared Miss Ellerby, "but I suppose you'll do what you want." She glanced at the door, and then jumped up as if in alarm. A girl who looked very young appeared, and by her side was Miss Abbott. The child was dressed in washed-out pink pyjamas and a cotton dressing-gown of the same colour. Her eyes looked huge, and her face was pale.

"What on earth are you doing up at this hour?" demanded Miss Ellerby.

"She woke, and discovered that Caroline was missing, and I found her outside," Miss Abbott said. "I thought you'd better have a word with her."

"Yes," agreed Miss Ellerby quietly. "Yes. Patricia, you are not to say a word about this, do you understand? Not a word."

"I–I won't, Miss Ellerby," the girl promised, "but–but is Caroline going to be all right?"

"Of course she is," the headmistress replied, and became quite mellow while reassuring the girl, before Miss Abbott took her off.

Twenty minutes later, Dawson was back, admitting that he had found nothing to help. Rollison took Eve out to the car. Miss Abbott had gone, yawning, to bed; there was no sign of Higgs, but outside there were at least a dozen men, half of them in uniform, and a lamp had been rigged up to light up the spot where Jeff had been run down. Dawson came out with Rollison, and asked a man:

"Any news from the hospital?"

"No, sir."

"Terrible business," Dawson said. "Terrible." He stepped with Rollison and Eve to the car, and shook hands and said sententiously: "I meant every word I said, Mrs Kane. We will protect your and your daughter's interests in every way we can."

"I'm sure you will," Eve said.

The clock on the instrument panel said ten minutes to four when Rollison moved off. The bright light behind him fell away, and he turned the corner which the small Hillman had turned a few hours ago. Almost immediately beyond it was a set of road signs, and he did not need Eve's directions. He turned left, for the London road, and soon they were in the starlit countryside, with the car moving very fast.

"If it were left to that awful man Dawson, I don't think I'd feel there was any hope at all," Eve said.

"I shouldn't underrate the Dawsons or the police in general," Rollison advised.

"They'll be so anxious to catch that driver that they'll tell the newspapers everything."

"They can handle the running down job simply as a case of hit-and-run," Rollison answered, "and they probably will. Eve, did you and the others recall anything which might help to tell what is behind all this?"

"No."

"Have you any idea at all where we might find your husband?"

"No. I would have told you."

"Do you know of anyone else who might know? This Leah, with whom he had trouble, for instance."

"I haven't any idea who he might be with or where he might be, but it looks as if he's taken Caroline out of the country, doesn't it?" Dread sounded in every word.

"Not on your life!" Rollison startled her by his vehemence.

"But, surely, the car at the airport—"

"That was the obvious place to leave it if anyone wanted to create the impression that Ralph had taken Caroline out of the country. Think of all the arguments against doing that. It's just possible, but extremely difficult, to get a drugged person on to an aircraft, and there aren't many drugs injected into the blood stream which put you out for a short period—usually they keep you under for hours. If you were really going to leave the country, would you make it so obvious? If your husband were going to kidnap Caroline, would he use a Colfax car and make it so clear that everyone would jump to the conclusion that he was responsible? The man you've told me about would have more sense than that."

There was new eagerness in Eve's voice.

"What are you trying to say?"

"I still don't think the evidence implicates your husband," Rollison said. "When you first came to see me it was to look for him, now it's to look for them both. We might find them together, too. If they're not in this country, I'll be astonished. Eve, do you know this Leah's address?"

"Why do you keep harping on her?"

"She's the only name I've got of anyone who might know where Ralph's gone, if he's in hiding."

"You just said that you didn't think he was involved, and that if we find one we might find both. You're not consistent. It isn't any use *guessing*."

"Tell me what else we can do," said Rollison grimly. "Tell me any other line we could follow, and I'll follow it. The police will cover all the obvious channels; we need to get on to something they're not likely to find. Leah, for instance, or any other of Ralph's girl friends."

"How do you think I know where to find them?" Eve demanded bitterly. "They weren't exactly social acquaintances."

"None of them?"

"What do you mean?"

"I mean, didn't you know any of them socially? Or, at least, don't you know where to find a single one of them?" When Eve didn't answer, he went on: "The police will work on the Colfax angle, they'll be after the people in the Super Snipe and the driver of the Hillman, so it will be wasting time for us to cover the same ground. Is there anyone who knew or knows Ralph who might be able to help?"

"I've thought about it until my head goes round and round, and I can't think of anyone," Eve answered, almost desperately.

"What about his men friends?"

"He had no real friends, just a lot of acquaintances."

"Surely someone knew him well?"

"Richard," Eve said, and it was the first time that she had used his Christian name, "not long after we were married Ralph told me that he would probably never have married me but for my money. He said that at the time he honestly thought that he was in love, but that it had been a mistake to tie himself down—he simply hadn't the right temperament. He told me he liked new faces, new people, and constant change. His work helped him—

travelling as a top-line advertising consultant, and meeting big business men from all parts of the world. In a way I felt almost sorry for him. He was never in one place for long, he seemed to be always chasing happiness. It didn't hurt any the less because I could see that he was driven to it by some inner compulsion, that he didn't live the way he did only for the sake of it. I honestly believe he tried in the first few years of our marriage; the years when Caroline was young, and when I was deeply in love with him. He just won't make close friends or permanent associations. He lives by himself and for himself. That's why I couldn't believe at first that he knew anything about this. I was sure he wouldn't want to saddle himself with Caroline. He was beginning to enjoy taking her out to dinner or luncheon, because she was becoming less of a schoolgirl and more of a young woman, but I can't believe he would want her with him all the time. I tell you that there's no one I can think of who might help, except possibly people at Colfax's, and I'm not even sure about them."

"Do you know this Leah's surname?"

Eve cried: "*Don't keep on about Leah!*"

"Eve—"

"Talk, talk, talk, that's all I hear, that's all that ever happens. I just can't stand it, I simply can't stand it!"

Rollison said: "I know, Eve." He drove for a few minutes, saw a lay-by sign, and pulled off the road. Eve was crying. He did not speak or touch her, and after a while she quietened. He heard her moving, saw that she was pushing her fingers through her hair. There was just the light of the dashboard to show her face when she looked at him.

"I'm sorry."

"I don't know how you kept up so long."

"It's not fair to start shouting at you." She dabbed at her eyes with a handkerchief. "You must have some reason for keeping on about Leah."

"She's the only person I've heard about who hated Ralph and might want to harm and to injure him, the only one with a possible motive. Is there anything at all you can tell me about her?"

Eve said slowly: "I don't know." He didn't ask her to explain the cryptic comment, and after a while she went on: "She once left a telephone number for him to call her back. It seemed to burn itself into my mind then, but I can't think of it now. It was Kensington 33412 or 44312— a number something like that. I'm sure there was a 3 and a 4 and a 1 in it, I'm sure it was Kensington. I wrote it down on a scrap of paper, and afterwards when I realised who it was, I threw it away."

Rollison said: "We can dial all likely permutations of 4, 3, 2, and 1, and we may strike lucky."

"It's such a slight chance. I didn't expect you to clutch at straws."

"You'd be surprised how many bricks a little straw will make," Rollison said mildly. He touched his pocket, and the ransom note, which he had not shown to anyone else. He would have taken it out then, but he did not want to add to Eve's tension. He started off again, and as dawn was breaking, reached the outskirts of London. The city seemed to stir itself from the stillness of the night.

At a little after half-past five he pulled up outside 22 Gresham Terrace, helped Eve out into the grey morning, and went upstairs. He opened the door and tip-toed in quietly, not wanting to disturb Jolly. He switched on the light, and it showed Eve looking washed-out and red-eyed; she would hate to think that he had seen her looking like this. He took her to the spare bedroom, said: "I keep this ready for out-of-town relations. You'll find everything you need, and the bathroom's next door. I'll bring in some tea and biscuits in ten minutes." He went back to the big room and stood looking at the Trophy Wall and the hangman's noose which was the most macabre of the exhibits. Then he took out the ransom note. It was in

pencilled block lettering, and he already knew it off by
heart.

"Get £20,000 ready, in cash. They must be old notes."

Was this simply a case of ransom?

How rich was Eve? Could she find such a huge sum?
Would anyone make a demand unless they felt sure that
she could? He picked up a magnifying glass, once used
to catch the sun's rays to start a fire which had burned
down a barn with two people in it, and went over the
note for prints: there was none. Gloved hands had held
this, the envelope, and the other card which he had in
his pocket. A clever amateur would think of it; and a
professional would not be careless enough to make a
present of his prints to the police.

He turned round—and saw an envelope addressed to
him in Jolly's clear handwriting, which as yet showed
little trace of *anno Domini*. So Jolly had been up; and he
should have been allowed to sleep the clock round.
Rollison opened the envelope and the fact that it was
sealed told him that Jolly had meant to impress him with
its seriousness.

It read:

"There was a telephone call at 3.45, sir.

"The caller, a man with a slightly coarse voice,
said that he now realises that the police will have to be
told something of what has happened, but that if they
are told of the cash request, the child will not be
returned. He said that he would be sending Mrs K.
further instructions.

"As there was nothing else I could reasonably do, I
decided to return to bed. Please call me immediately
you are in—I shall be perfectly well."

Rollison put the note down, looked sardonically at the
Trophy Wall, and said *sotto voce*: "All very calm and
under control." He put the note in his pocket, and went
into the kitchen. "They're very sure of themselves, but

they shouldn't have run Jeff down." He made tea, took biscuits from the larder and carried them into the spare room. There was no nonsense about Eve Kane: she was in bed, lying back on the pillows, wearing a borrowed pale blue nightdress; her eyes looked lack-lustre.

"I don't want anything," she said. "I saw some veronal tablets in the bathroom and took one—if I don't get some sleep, I shall be no use at all."

"You'll sleep like a top."

"We'll see," she said, and when he turned to the door and had his hand on the switch, she said: "Rolly, it's quite impossible for me to say how grateful I am."

"Forget it," he said. "Good night, Eve." He turned out the light, went into the passage, and closed the door slowly. He moved away, as slowly. She was not truly beautiful and she had probably never looked more dishevelled than she did now, but there was a quality in her which caught and held him. He had never felt quite like this before. He grinned at himself, and went into his own bedroom, stripped, put on pyjamas and slipped into bed; it had been a waste of time making that tea. He needed a few hours' sleep, and it wouldn't be much use trying to trace this Leah too early in the morning. Kensington 33412, or 44312, or—

He began to count permutations as one might count sheep, until eventually he dropped off.

The telephone bell woke him.

C

8

KENSINGTON 33412

"ROLLISON here," Rollison said gruffly.

"Hold on, please, Superintendent Marshall wants you," a girl said with a brightness which seemed hideous in Rollison's ears. He sat up in bed, one eye open, and squinted at the bedside clock; it was twenty minutes past eight. He hoped the ringing hadn't disturbed Jolly or Eve. He held on for what seemed a long time, and no one else moved in the flat. Then Marshall came on: "Rolly?"

"Don't you ever go home?"

"I'm on my way, but I thought you'd like a word first," said Marshall, gruffly: he might have been talking after a night's rest, not after a long spell of duty. "We traced the drug in that needle. Morphia. No way of being sure how much, but a normal dose would put a girl under for eight or nine hours. We've got a line of sorts on that Super Snipe, too. It was driven to the airport by a Teddy boy type, thirty-ish, on his own. He walked out of the car park and wasn't noticed after that. He didn't go to one of the loading platforms or the customs bays, and he certainly didn't have a girl with him. Shouldn't think Caroline Kane went off from London airport; that was a blind. You listening?"

"And marvelling," Rollison said. "Thanks very much, Nick."

"Only hope we can find that kid," Marshall said. "We haven't traced the Hillman—it was a bad time of night, and too many roads weren't covered. That shocking bore Dawson thinks he had a tyre print taken from Jeff's shirt, but that's the only hope there."

66

Rollison was suddenly wide awake.

"Any news of Jeff?"

"Multiple internal injuries and fractured arm and hip. No more than a fifty-fifty chance, the hospital says, but they'll pull him through if it's possible. Have you got anything else?"

"No," Rollison said, and half wished that there was no need to lie. "There's something you can do for me, though."

"What is it?"

"Leave a message to whoever is taking over from you that I might want to find out an address starting from a telephone number."

"It's Bill Grice," Marshall said. "Doesn't he always eat out of your hand?"

Rollison said: "Never known it yet," but he felt more cheerful, for he knew Grice well and was sure that Grice would help in every way he could. "Thanks."

"What's this about a telephone number?"

"One Mrs Kane remembers her husband using a lot."

"Oh. Well, I wish you luck," Marshall said, and then broke off; the sound which followed seemed as if he had been caught with a gargantuan yawn. ". . . ugh," he finished. "Sorry. Good-bye."

He rang off.

Jolly was asleep; and so was Eve. Her back was turned towards Rollison when he looked in, and the bedclothes were drawn right up to her shoulders, in spite of the sticky warmth of the morning. He found himself wondering what her husband would say if he came here and saw her. Rollison had a cold bath, felt much better for it, munched biscuits and drank tea as he sat at his desk, the telephone in front of him. The first number that Eve had given him was Kensington 33412, and there was at least a chance that her memory was better than she realised. At ten minutes past nine exactly, he dialled the number.

There was a long pause, and he began to wonder if it were an office which didn't open until later; or an empty flat; or even a telephone call box. He was on the point of giving up when there was a break in the ringing sound, and a woman answered:

"Marple Guest House."

"Where?" asked Rollison, startled.

"Marple *Guest* House," the woman said, and she sounded breathless. "Who do you want?"

"Is Leah there, please?" asked Rollison, and was answered almost before he had finished speaking.

"It's no use asking me to wake Leah, she wasn't in until after two, and she's like a log until ten or eleven every morning, anyway. Can I give her a message?"

"No," Rollison said, his heart thumping. "I'll call again."

He put down the receiver, very slowly, and as the bell went *ting!* he heard a rustle of movement in the door behind him. He turned. Eve was standing in the doorway, a pale blue dressing-gown loosely round her, her hair dishevelled and yet attractive, her face as attractive although she had on no make-up. She was holding the dressing-gown together at the waist.

"What is it?" she demanded eagerly. "Why are you smiling?"

"There's a Leah still at Kensington 33412," Rollison said quietly. "The first number I tried. That's the kind of luck that needs following up. I'm going to see her alone. I want you to take it easy here, and when Jolly wakes make him telephone Dr Welling, or telephone yourself. Will you?"

"Yes, of course. Dr Welling?"

"Yes. Thanks," said Rollison. "And there's negative news, too." He told her about the airport story, but not about the morphia, and he saw the glow of hope in her eyes.

.   .   .   .

At a quarter to eleven, Rollison reached a corner house in a quiet Kensington Street—Marple Street. A small sign fastened to the wall by the porch, which was supported by two rounded pillars, read: *Marple Guest House.* The brown front door needed painting, and it stood ajar. He opened it wide and stepped into a narrow hall. A vacuum cleaner was buzzing somewhere upstairs. The hall was papered a faded blue with red roses on it, there were a few old prints in cheap frames, a big mirror which was badly speckled, a hall stand, a baize-covered board festooned with notices of nearby cinemas and a few West End theatres and, the thing which Rollison was really glad to see, an *In—Out* board. In all there were about fifteen names, and opposite each was a number, presumably a room number, and alongside this the word *In* or *Out*, which could be changed from one to the other by sliding a small marker. There were two showing *In*—a Mr Carter and a Miss Soloman. Leah and Soloman went together well enough.

It would be Leah Soloman who had been out late the night before—late enough to have driven from Hapley after taking the girl away from the station.

"There couldn't be that much luck," Rollison said softly.

The vacuum cleaner stopped, and he could hear his own breathing. He waited for footsteps, but heard none; and the cleaner started again. Miss Soloman's room was 7. He went up the stairs, which were covered with a strip of carpet already threadbare in places. The house was clean enough, and the furniture and the banisters seemed to be polished; it was good third rate. He reached a landing and saw four doors closed, a bathroom door open; the doors were marked 3 to 6. He went up the next flight of stairs, turned along a landing, and saw room 7, straight in front of him; the numeral 7 was a metal one, screwed into the door.

The vacuum was on the floor above, and seemed much

louder. He wanted it to go on. He took out a penknife which was a little fatter than most, and selected a blade which police would have frowned on but which would have made a burglar's eyes glisten; it was a simple pick-lock. He felt quite safe to use it under cover of the noise of the vacuum cleaner, and twisted it freely. He felt it push out the key on the other side, then felt the resistance, twisted—and as the lock went back the vacuum cleaner stopped, and the *click!* sounded startlingly loud.

Rollison stood quite still. The sounds above his head suggested that the cleaner was being pushed along manually; and then footsteps sounded immediately overhead, as if the woman with the machine had stepped into the passage. He turned the handle of room 7, and thrust; if Leah Soloman bolted her door, he would have to try again, and—

She didn't.

The door opened, and he stepped into a shadowy room, with blinds drawn at big windows; and the windows were probably closed, because the room had a heavy smell, of body warmth and cheap scent and stale tobacco smoke. He closed the door swiftly and the room seemed much darker. He picked up the fallen key, inserted and turned it, and the lock clicked. He dropped the key into his pocket as someone started coming down the stairs, treading very heavily.

He heard a creaking sound, and from the bed which was against the wall on his right a woman said in a squeaky voice:

"That you, Max?"

"If you don't want to get badly hurt, keep quiet," Rollison said roughly.

The woman in bed was too far away from him to put a hand over her mouth, and there was nothing to stop her from calling for help, unless this frightened her into silence. He heard the creaking much more loudly, and saw her struggling to sit up. She was breathing very hard.

The light from the window was kind to her, for he could make out little more than her shape. The vacuum cleaner thumped on the floor just outside the room, and a woman clumped along, pushing it.

The woman in the bed drew in a deep breath, as if she were going to scream for help.

"*Quiet, or I'll bring the police,*" Rollison whispered.

She didn't cry out. The footsteps began thumping down the stairs again. The woman in the bed had not moved, and now that Rollison was getting accustomed to the light, he could see her fair hair falling to her shoulders, and remembered Smart's description, of a small waisted, balloon-bosomed blonde.

"Who–who are you?" she managed to ask squeakily.

"Just sit there, and keep quiet," Rollison ordered. He went across to the window, and raised the blind a little; beyond it was a net curtain, so he could let in a little light without the risk of being seen. He let the blind up; it rolled viciously round its roller, and shed bright light on Leah Soloman.

For the second time that morning, he saw a woman at her worst who yet stood up well under scrutiny. Silky blonde hair was this one's saving grace, but she had rosy cheeks and bright eyes and a fresh complexion; she wasn't any more than twenty-two or three. Her small mouth suggested that she could be spiteful, but just now it was taut and her eyes were rounded in genuine fear. She sat bolt upright. She wore a yellow pyjama suit which stretched very tightly, too tightly for comfort, he thought; and she looked like a little high-breasted pigeon. It was almost certain that she also had a small waist.

"*What do you want?*"

"Where did you take Caroline Kane?" asked Rollison, moving towards her as he spoke. He would be able to judge from her reaction whether she recognised the name or not: and in a moment he was quite sure. She threw up her hands, as if in dread.

"Well, where?" he demanded. He drew near enough to spring forward and slap a hand across her mouth if she looked likely to scream, but he thought that she was paralysed with fear. "Tell me and be quick about it, and I'll forget you had anything to do with it. Where is she?"

"It's no use asking me," the girl gasped. She was breathing hissingly now. "I don't know where they took her. We brought her to London and handed her over. That was all we had to do."

"So that was all you had to do," said Rollison heavily. He felt a sense of anti-climax, because she admitted that so quickly. It was too easy, and experience had taught him that whenever a solution seemed too easy, it was time to prepare for the unexpected snag. He moved to the side of the bed and stood looking down at her; and he saw her dart a glance towards the door, as if she were sure that it would open and that help would come. He stood with his fingers crooked, ready to close them round her throat, and went on softly: "Who did you hand her over to?"

"I don't know who it was," Leah gasped. "There was a man in a car, but I didn't see him; it was pitch dark. I don't know where she's gone."

"Don't you?" asked Rollison, very softly, and the glitter in his eyes frightened her, for she thrust her hands out towards him, palms downwards, and pressed back against the pillows.

That was the moment when Rollison heard the sound at the door.

9

REASON TO KILL

It might be the woman with the vacuum cleaner, but Rollison believed that she walked too heavily to reach this door without making some noise; and there had been none until the handle began to turn. It was a good thing he had locked it. He whispered: "Don't make a sound," while Leah stared at the door as if towards salvation; if she cried out, even a locked door would not help, and only fear of his hovering hands would keep her quiet.

The handle stopped moving.

The stealthiness of this told Rollison that whoever stood outside had some reason to catch Leah unawares, and possibly knew that he was here. What would he do when the door would not move?

The door opened.

It moved very slowly, and Leah saw it, and caught her breath. So there were two keys—a pass key, of course. This might be the woman—or the 'Max' Leah had named. There was brightness from the landing window, and a shadow appeared. Rollison moved a little away from the bed, so that he could see both Leah and the door. He felt oddly defenceless. He had a mental vision of the driver of the small car running Jeff down with the cold-bloodedness of a killer. He had no weapon. He found himself wishing almost desperately that he had, and looked round for something he could use. On the dressing-table there were the usual oddments and a heavy looking hair brush, but it was just out of reach.

The shadow was short—or distorted.

Leah gasped: "Max, be careful, be careful!"

On the last word, the door crashed back against the

wall, and a short man stood on the threshold. He had a jacket, with absurdly wide shoulders, a turnip-shaped face, and jet black hair; this was almost certainly the man whom Smart the railway porter had seen. With his back to the door, what light there was fell on his face; his eyes seemed to glitter. He kept his right hand in the pocket of his coat, thrusting it forward, as if he were pretending that he had a gun; but it might not be pretence. The warning meant nothing to him; there was no hint of fear in his manner as he stared at Rollison, came forward, and hooked the door to with his foot. It slammed.

"How long has he been here?" he demanded.

"He–he's only just come; he woke me up. He—"

"What did he want to know?" asked the man named Max.

"About–about that girl last night."

It was done deliberately, of course, in an attempt to unnerve Rollison, and it would have unnerved a great number of people. It made Rollison very wary indeed, for this Max talked to the girl as if no one else were present.

"Did he?" Max said. "What did you tell him?"

"Nothing! Nothing. I wouldn't—"

The man stepped forward.

"What did you tell him?" he demanded again.

He had a surprisingly pleasant voice, and as he finished, he smiled. Fine white teeth seemed to light up his face and there was an amused-looking gleam in his eyes, too; seen in different circumstances, he would have seemed attractive and pleasant. He moved softly and without any physical effort, in a gliding motion. He kept his right hand in his pocket, and that side of him was closer to Rollison, at whom he had not even glanced.

Leah was obviously more frightened of him than of Rollison. She clutched the bedclothes in front of her as if they would give some kind of physical protection, her pouty little mouth was trembling, and she could not get words out.

If he helped her, Rollison thought, she might be useful

later on. He ought to say: 'She told me nothing.' Against that there was the undoubted fact that Max was ignoring him simply to force him to speak first; these were tactics meant to dominate, and would often succeed. The problem was to decide quickly whether to lie and so win Leah's favour later, or whether to wait and let Max break the ice. Before he could decide, Max said:

"Tell me, Leah," in a soft, persuasive voice, and she was so frightened that she burst out:

"I told him we'd handed her over to another man. I couldn't tell him any more, I didn't know who it was!"

"No, you didn't—" Max began, still pleasantly.

For the first time, Max turned to face Rollison.

He was certainly short; no more than five feet five or six. The cut of the coat might make him seem much more broad-shouldered than he was; certainly it made him seem shorter. He raised one thick black eyebrow slightly, and said:

"Sure, I know."

"Who was it?" asked Rollison mildly.

Max looked surprised; and then his smile flashed, and he looked as if he were genuinely amused.

"Who wants to know?"

"I do."

"Who are you?"

"A friend of Mrs Kane?"

"I wondered about that," Max said. "Mrs Kane has some remarkable friends." He looked Spanish, Italian or Southern French; he looked like a Teddy boy; he looked as if he really belonged to the street corners of Soho—and he spoke like an English public school boy, behaving rather as if all this were a game he found amusing. "Tell me more, stranger—what's your name?"

"Shall we skip that?" suggested Rollison.

Max smiled again, a little more tensely. "Ask Leah if you can skip anything I want to know," he advised. "Tell him, Leah. Do we ever skip anything?"

"No," the girl gasped.

"You see," said Max, and raised that thick eyebrow again. "So what's your name?"

There were moments to force an issue, and this was not one of them. Rollison smiled faintly, and felt the quickening beat of his pulse, and a forbidding sense of apprehension. It was easy to understand why Leah was so frightened of Max, less easy to understand how Ralph Kane could have associated with her.

"I'm a patient man," Max remarked.

"Sometimes you have to be," Rollison said, and dropped his right hand to his pocket. As he did so, there was a transformation in the other man; a swift change of expression, a glitter instead of a gleam in his eyes, a darting movement of his right hand; and a small automatic, the real thing, showed in that hand and pointed at Rollison.

"Keep your hands away from your pocket."

"Max," said Rollison gently, "guns make a noise. At least three people know that I came to see Leah. Don't be hasty." He continued to put his right hand to his pocket, but now he felt a thumping of his heart, in case Max ignored his warning. The girl was sitting bolt upright, and seemed to be trying to stifle her sobs. Without haste of any kind, Rollison took a card from his pocket, identical with the one he had given to the police at Hapley. He held this between his middle and forefinger, and flicked it lightly; it fell on the floor between Max and the bed. "My card," Rollison said.

There was a moment's pause; for the first time, Max seemed uncertain what to do. Then he smiled again. The smile wasn't so free as before, nor so charming, but at least he had taken head of the warning, and there was a smaller risk that he would shoot.

"Leah, pick that up and bring it to me," he said. "I don't think I should trust this joker too far."

"B-B-but I—"

"You haven't got any clothes on, but why worry about that?" demanded Max. "Get it."

"No, I—"

"Leah," said Max very softly, "we don't want any more misunderstandings, do we?"

She gave a little sob, and pushed back the bedclothes. Rollison caught a glimpse of a white, plump thigh; she had on the pyjama jacket but not the trousers. He turned away from her towards the window, which overlooked the street that he could just see at the side of the blinds. His back was towards Max and the girl. He heard the bed springs creak, heard the little thumps of her footsteps, a moment's pause, and then a resounding slap, of palm on plump flesh. She gave a little squeal, and a moment later scrambled back into bed.

"Now that's what I call a real gentleman," said Max, mockingly, and Rollison turned round to see the girl drawing the clothes up almost to her neck. Max was glancing down at the card and the man without a face. He looked intrigued, but nothing in his expression suggested that he recognised it. "A real Toff," he went on. "I should think—"

He stopped.

His smile disappeared, he frowned and so brought a deep furrow just above the nose, drawing those thick jet black eyebrows together. The name had registered, after all, and it did not give him pleasure. He held the gun in one hand and the card in the other, and then said flatly:

"*The* Toff, are you?"

Rollison shrugged. "What's in a name?"

"Well, well," said Max, but he had lost a great deal of his buoyancy, and that was a good thing to see. "I didn't think I would ever meet the great Toff in person. Leah, this is your lucky morning. This is one of the British aristocracy's noble scions, as well as being a friend of Scotland Yard. Don't say you never heard of the Toff."

He was giving himself time to recover from the shock.

"I–I–I think I've heard the name somewhere," Leah gabbled.

"You need a better publicity man, someone hasn't heard of you," Max said to Rollison. He moistened his lips, and then put his gun back in his pocket but kept his hand in his pocket, too. "So you're a friend of Mrs Kane."

"Her problems are my problems," Rollison declared earnestly.

"That could be one of your mistakes," Max retorted. "I get it now, though. I thought that name Rollison was familiar, but I didn't—" He broke off, and for the first time since he had taken the card his smile was really broad. "Toff, I think this might work out better than either of us expected; this could be the solution to our little problem. How much do the police know about Caroline's disappearance?"

"All of it."

"Do they know about the request for money?"

"No."

"Your friend Mrs Kane is a very wealthy woman. Did you know that?"

"I've heard it rumoured."

"It's a fact," Max said. "Twenty thousand pounds won't make much difference to her. What do you think of people who can say good-bye to twenty thousand pounds and not be worried about it? Don't you think they ought to share some of the cash?"

Rollison made no comment.

"So all you have to do is to collect the money from her and bring it to me," said Max, and now his smile was really expansive. "She needn't be worried any more. I get the money—and you get Caroline Kane shorn of a lock of a hair but otherwise sound in wind, limb and memory. We'll have to make arrangements by which we can be sure you won't cheat; but a gentleman who turns his back on a lady wouldn't do such a thing, would he?"

"You might try to find out," said Rollison.

"It wouldn't be good for you or for sweet Caroline if I found out that you did try to cheat," said Max, and the tension was back in his eyes and at his lips. "Don't get me wrong, Toff. I know what I'm doing. I know there's a big risk. But twenty thousand pounds is worth taking a risk for. You might manage to put me in jail, but you could be absolutely sure of one thing: before I went to jail, Caroline would have a very bad time. She's a nice girl, I should think. Her mother wouldn't like to think that she'd learned all about life the hard way, before she died."

Rollison sensed that this man was not talking for the sake of talking: that what he had threatened, he would try to carry out. It was an evil thought. The fact that he understood how evil probably showed in his face, for Max relaxed again, and his smile looked more pleasant.

"So how about going and making the arrangements?" he suggested. "That way it will be nice and friendly and pleasant for everyone concerned. I get the money, you get the girl, the Toff has triumphed again, and no one is any worse off. Right?"

After a long pause, Rollison said:

"Isn't there one little thing you've forgotten?"

"Don't tell me that you are going to talk about right for right's sake, the triumph of virtue, and—"

"I was thinking of Ralph Kane."

"And where does Ralph Kane come into this?" inquired Max, as if with interest. He looked round at Leah, and asked in the same light voice: "You haven't seen your old friend Ralph again lately, have you? It's a funny thing," he went on, "but if Ralph Kane had treated Leah properly this probably wouldn't have happened. Would it, Leah? Have you seen him?"

"I haven't seen him for six months," Leah declared eagerly. "Honestly I haven't. God's truth."

10

TRUTH?

Rollison was looking at Leah as she answered, and the reply came without a moment's hesitation; but it was extremely likely that she was lying. She looked prettier now; surreptitiously she had tidied her hair, and although the flush of sleep had gone, she had a complexion quite like roses, and her eyes seemed brighter and bluer; it was easy to understand how a man could be attracted by her— but would a man like Ralph Kane?

He had been.

"Ralph Kane never had two pennies to rub together," said the man named Max, lightly. "If he had, we would have got all we wanted from him, and it was only when I realised that he hadn't anything to pay with that I began to think about his wife. After all, what belongs to a wife is also her husband's, or it should be in a happy family! So forget Ralph. Supposing you go and talk to Mrs Kane, and advise her that the wise thing to do is to pay the money. I'll telephone you at"— Max flicked a glance at the gold wrist-watch on his left hand—"half-past twelve, shall we say? Or doesn't that allow time enough? Make it half-past one. There will still be an hour and a half before the banks close. I'll tell you where to bring the money. All right?"

"What makes you so sure that I won't bring the police?"

"Oh, I'm not sure," said Max airily. "I told you, a man has to take some risks when he's playing for high stakes, and my risk is that you'll be a stiff-necked so-and-so, and do what you think is the right thing." He put a haw-haw tone into his voice with complete aplomb. "You and Mrs K. have to take risks, too. She has to risk losing her daughter. You have to risk losing your life."

80

He smiled.

Rollison said: "I'm not sure that it is a risk," but he had very little doubt that this man was not bluffing. One thing became more obvious every minute: in Max there was something of the cold-bloodedness of the driver of the small car. Had he been that driver? Rollison had seldom known a man make him feel so uneasy; he had often been on edge because of fear of death or pain, but never because of innuendo and threat. He did not fully understand his own reaction, although at the back of his mind he knew that his fears were not for himself, but for Eve.

Above everything else, he wanted to help her.

"You just have to gamble on it," Max went on.

"I suppose so," Rollison conceded.

"Toff, I don't want to detain you any longer," Max declared. For the first time he took his hand from his pocket, without the gun, as if to show that he was sure he had nothing more to fear. "You can send for the police, you can even bring them here. I think I should get away, but whether I did or not, Caroline Kane would never show up alive again. That's the kind of gamble you'd be taking!" He gave his broadest smile. "Be close by the telephone at half-past one."

Rollison hesitated, and then said: "I will be."

"That's my boy!"

Rollison saw the glint in the dark eyes, telling that Max felt quite sure he had won. Max actually turned towards Leah, as if Rollison no longer mattered, but he had that curiously cat-like movement, and would swing round if Rollison made the slightest false move. Rollison stepped to the door, hesitated, then turned round and said:

"How do I know you'll have the girl with you?"

"You don't, do you?" said Max blandly. "You just have to take my word for it that I'll hand over the girl in exchange for twenty thousand pounds. It's nearly eleven o'clock," he went on. "You haven't a lot of time to work in."

Now he turned his back on Rollison, but in the wall near him was a mirror, and he could see any move that Rollison made. Rollison put a hand on the door, opened it, and stepped outside. Max, probably beaming, said something to Leah in a low-pitched voice. Leah made a gurgle of sound in reply.

Rollison stepped outside, closed the door, and went downstairs, walking rather heavily, as if he hated being forced to leave. He reached the first landing, and almost opposite him was the open door of the bathroom. He passed this, reached the front passage, and went out into the street. He was quite sure that Max would be watching from the window. He glanced up, and saw that the gap between the side of the blind and the window was wider, and also saw a hand pulling it back. He went straight to the corner of the street. The Rolls-Bentley was being admired by a middle-aged man, who glanced at him and said:

"Beautiful job, isn't it?"

"Eh?" asked Rollison. "Oh, the car. Yes, isn't it?" He saw the man's expression change to one of startled surprise when he got in. "Good morning." He started the engine and eased off the brake at one and the same moment, shot the car forward towards the far end of the street, turned the corner to the left, went left again, and pulled up close to that corner; round it was Marple Street. He got out of the car and slammed the door, then half-walked, half-ran, towards the guest house. By keeping close to the front of the houses there was little risk of being seen, even if Max was alive to the possibility that he would double back. Max wouldn't miss much, but having seen him leave the house and turn the corner, he probably thought that he had won without a real fight.

The front of the guest house was still open.

Rollison went in, bent down and slipped off his shoes, and hurried silently up the stairs. As he neared number 7, he heard a sound that surprised him, and he paused on the landing. The sound was repeated: laughter. He drew on his shoes and stepped towards the door. Max and Leah were laughing as if at the best joke in the world; Max was nothing if not a character. The girl began to squeal, breathless with laughter, and gradually words formed themselves. "Don't, Max. Oh, Max, don't! Max, don't!" She was almost hysterical, and there was little doubt that Max was tickling her. This might be exactly the right moment to go in, they were so preoccupied; but there would be a restriction of movement inside the room. Rollison stood flat against the wall so that when the door opened he would be able to stretch out a hand and grab Max; or stretch out a leg, and trip him. The laughter was now a series of gasps, the kind which was almost agonising.

Then, while Leah was gasping for breath, Max said:

"Okay, Leah, I'll give you a break. But next time don't let me catch you with your pants down." He seemed quite good-humoured and on top of the world. "I don't think Rollison will come and see you again, but if he does you don't know a thing more."

"Well, I don't anyway," Leah managed to say.

"That's right, you don't," agreed Max.

Undoubtedly, he was smiling that beaming smile. Rollison heard him come across the room towards the door, and flattened himself against the wall so that there was no risk of being seen when the door opened, unless Max was still suspicious and wary, and peered out before he stepped outside. There would still be time to catch him before he could take any action—unless he carried his gun at the ready. He might do that. Rollison felt the now familiar sense of apprehension, admitting to himself that the next move was quite unpredictable; this man knew all the tricks, and might have one up his sleeve.

Max opened the door.

He turned and waved to Leah, and kissed his fingers at her. Then he stepped outside, pulling the door as he did so, and it was firmly closed when Rollison lunged, caught his right wrist and thrust it upwards, forcing him to turn round. Then Rollison dipped his hand into his pocket and drew out the automatic. Once that was in his own pocket, his tension eased. Max had drawn in one hissing breath, but made no attempt to struggle; there was no doubt that he knew Rollison might break his arm.

"Downstairs," Rollison ordered. "Don't try to run away." He thrust the man forward a little, and Max stepped out awkwardly, careful not to jolt his arm. They went down without being seen, but as they reached the hall, a door at the end of the front passage opened, and a woman said:

"Oh! You gave me quite a shock." She could see Rollison's back, but very little of Max. "Did–did you want someone?"

Max said: "It's okay, Mrs Bottley, this is a friend of mine." He sounded natural enough and the answer satisfied the woman. The front door was open. He went out, Rollison still gripping his arm. Almost certainly he told himself that Rollison would not keep that hold on him when they were in the street, and that would be his chance to get away.

"Max," Rollison said.

"Toff," said Max.

"Don't run, and don't do anything foolish," urged Rollison. "Apart from the fact that you might break your arm, the police would be very glad to see you. You killed a policeman last night."

"I wasn't within fifty miles of Hapley when that copper was run down," Max said, "and I can prove it." He paused for a moment, and then went on: "So he died."

Rollison didn't know for sure, but said: "Yes."

"That's too bad."

"You'll soon find out how bad it is."

"Toff," said Max, "I don't know what's on your mind, but let me give you a little information." He was moving forward quickly, arm still held behind him and thrust upwards, so that although they looked as if they were walking peculiarly only someone very close by could see what was really happening. "It's about Caroline Kane."

"Go on."

"She won't have a chance at all if you take me to the police."

"Perhaps I think I ought to call your bluff."

"It's not bluff," Max insisted. "But why don't you try it? And then why don't you talk to Mrs Kane afterwards? Tell her you didn't mean to sign her Carrie's death warrant—such a nasty death, too—and see how much that helps. There were some things that Ralph Kane helped us with, Toff. He told us how much his wife loved his daughter. What do they call it? Maternal fixation, or something. You ever noticed how often a mother or a father dotes on a child if ma and pa don't exactly hit it off?"

Rollison said mildly: "Max, you're going to take me to Caroline."

"Not on your life," retorted Max.

They reached the corner, and the Rolls-Bentley stood facing them. Rollison went on thrusting the man towards it, and said: "Open the door." After a moment's hesitation, Max did so, and said:

"Well, well, what's it like to be rich? How do you spend your money, Toff? I'd like to find out the best way, and I've a feeling that you know. Do you want me to get into this piece of opulence?"

"Yes."

"Believe it or not, this is the first time I have ever sat in a Rolls-Royce or Bentley of any kind," said Max, as if with reverence. When Rollison released his arm, he eased it and moved his shoulder gingerly, got in, and leaned back; there was a seraphic expression on his face as he closed his eyes. "My," he breathed. "This is really what it's like to be in the money. Did I ever tell you that I intend to be rich before I've finished?"

Rollison locked the door, which was on the passenger's side, and went round to the driving wheel. Max had made no attempt to move, and he was smiling raptly when Rollison sat next to him, and put a hand on the wheel.

"Toff," Max went on, very gently. "Don't let heroics force you into a serious mistake. You live a comfortable kind of life. Any man who can run a car like this and has an address in Mayfair must know all about the good times. Why spoil it? Why try to build up your reputation any more? You're in the money and Mrs Kane's in the money. Put me and my friends in the money, and you'll get the girl back so we can forget all about it. Why don't you?"

Rollison said: "Because if you get away with it this time, you'll try it again."

"Not on the same people, Toff, and you needn't know anything about the next time! Twenty thousand pounds is exactly the right sum for me to start with. I know how to work after that. Leah's a bigger help than you might think. Know what Leah does? She finds my fools, the rich fools, the Ralph Kanes of this world, and I separate them from some of their riches. We thought that Kane was well heeled, but soon found that he had the next best thing—his wife. With twenty thousand in the kitty, so to speak, we can manage quite nicely. Don't make it difficult and don't make Mrs Kane a bereaved mother. Be sensible. Tell her to pay up."

He was talking earnestly while Rollison was driving towards Kensington High Street, and trying to decide the most effective thing to do. He could take Max to the flat, but it would be impossible to deal with him if Eve were still there. In his heart he knew exactly what Eve would want to do: pay the money. Well, if Eve could afford it, what were the arguments against? The child would be all right, at least he could make sure of that. There was logic in Max's arguments, and Max knew exactly what he was doing—

Rollison forced the ideas away almost in dismay. A policeman badly injured if not dead, Max and Leah left to prey upon fools, Max even more cocky if he got away with this: it was impossible to think of advising Eve to pay.

But she would want to.

"While you're making up your mind," Max said, "do you mind if I have a cigarette?" He took out cigarettes, used the dashboard cigar lighter as if it were a new toy, puffed with relish, and then went on: "There's a particularly bad mistake you could make, Toff. You might think that I work alone. Just at the moment, I imagine, a colleague of mine is having a cosy little chat with Caroline's mother."

11

COSY LITTLE CHAT

WHEN the door closed behind Richard Rollison, Eve Kane stood looking at the Trophy Wall for a few moments, saw sunlight from the window glint on the glass of a small cabinet filled with phials containing powder, presumably poison, and stepped quickly to the window. By pressing close against it, she could just see the pavement outside the front door of this house. Almost at once, Rollison appeared, and she watched him turn right, and walk with long, easy strides towards the car; a man with complete confidence in himself, and obviously superbly fit. But neither of those things explained the way she felt about him; there was no easy explanation, but it was a simple fact that she felt more at ease with him than she had ever done with a man—even her own husband.

She would have hated Ralph to see her as she had been when she had come into this room and faced Rollison; it had not occurred to her to think twice about Rollison seeing her. If anything was absolutely certain it was that he would do his utmost to help her, and would not miss a chance.

She turned towards that remarkable wall. Anywhere else, it would have seemed showy, even ostentatious; in this otherwise beautifully furnished room it should look like that. Instead, it was 'right'; even the top hat on the peg close to the ceiling had a kind of jauntiness. She saw a hole in it, and then realised that it was a bullet hole.

Had Rolly been wearing the hat when that hole had been made?

She looked at other trophies; at knives, guns, poisons, rope, wire, hammers—some obviously weapons for crimes of violence, that 'blunt instrument' so often read about. Others had some association with murder and violence which it was not easy to grasp: the nylon stocking, for instance; some chickens' feathers; a white wedding veil; a Salvation Army hat placed in the centre of them all. She sensed the romance and the excitement and the danger which those souvenirs told of, and they gave her a deep, helpful feeling of confidence.

Here was all the evidence that Rollison knew exactly what he was doing.

What had he asked her to do?

Have Jolly telephone the doctor, or telephone herself, of course; but what was the doctor's name? She ought to have remembered it. Webber, Well–Welling? She hurried to the desk, hesitated, then opened a drawer, and was lucky to find a small card index at the front of it, marked *addresses*. She found a card for Dr G. Welling, and a Mayfair telephone number. She dialled, and when a girl answered, said:

"I've a message for Dr Welling from Mr Rollison."

"One moment, please . . ." After a brief pause a man came on the line, and Eve explained simply that Rollison's man was ill, and the doctor promised: "I'll be over within the hour." Eve rang off, and went into the kitchen, hesitated, and then opened the door of a room just along a narrow passage. She heard a man breathing heavily as she stepped inside. An elderly man was lying on his back, rather high on spotlessly white pillows. His cheeks were colourless, and his lips seemed pale, too. She went across to him, and realised that he was really ill; he probably had a very high temperature. There was sweat on his forehead and his upper lip. If she wiped that off she might wake him, and it would be better if he could stay as he was until the doctor arrived; but she wished she had come in here first; she could have made it sound more urgent.

This new anxiety preoccupied her. She told herself she would call Dr Welling again if he were even a minute

late, and then began to speculate about Rollison's
expedition.

She found herself thinking of this Leah, whom she had
heard but never seen; a girl with a rather high-pitched
almost common voice, sounding both angry and venge-
ful. Just what had her husband done, Eve found herself
wondering bitterly. Then she faced the fact that he was
still missing and Caroline was missing, and fear came over
her like a great blinding sheet. She could not stay here
and do nothing.

Why do nothing? She had plenty to do. She hurried to
the bathroom, washed, dressed quickly, noting on the
surface of her mind that Rollison had everything a woman
required here; was it all kept for relations? Did that
matter? He was a bachelor, and bachelors had a licence
which married men should not claim. She clenched her
hands at the thought of the unhappy years, the gradual
awakening to the realisation that, when Ralph was away,
he was seldom alone. Time had acclimatised her to it,
and there had been nothing between them, as man and
wife, for many years; they kept up appearances for
Caroline's sake, because Caroline had so idolised her
father. Ralph had known that was the reason why Eve
stayed with him.

Now he had done this to Caroline—

Was that fair? Did he know what had happened? Was
it coincidence that he had disappeared first?

Eve simply did not know.

She made herself some tea and toast, and when she had
finished, half an hour had passed since the telephone call.
If the doctor didn't come early she would call him again;
she ought to have telephoned again immediately after she
had seen Rollison's man. Jolly. Jolly—Rolly. She wondered if she ought to look in at the sick man again, but did
not. She opened her handbag and took out a photograph
of Caroline, a smiling, happy Caroline with a hockey
stick held in front of her, a mop of hair untidy.

She closed her eyes—and as she stood there, a bell rang. Was that the front door? Dr Welling?

She put the photograph away and hurried into the lounge hall. It would be the doctor, of course, here ahead of time. She fumbled with the door, which seemed to have a special kind of lock, got it open at last—and saw a rather short man standing and looking at her with a tentative kind of smile. She did not think that he was Dr Welling; for one thing, he carried no bag. He was very dark, and did not look English, an Italian, perhaps, or—

She remembered the description of the man who had been at Hapley Station.

The man smiled more broadly, and showed flashing white teeth. In a way he was good looking, although his forehead was very wide and broad, giving his face a round appearance. He wore no hat. His jet black hair was cut very short, and his thick black eyebrows looked as if they had been trimmed, to keep them short and to make them grow thicker. He had a rather sallow complexion, but a good skin. All of these things made a swift impression on Eve, while her heart thumped with fear.

He inquired: "Mrs Kane?"

She could hardly find the words. "Yes, I am."

"May I speak to you, please?" His English was good, but had a faint accent; Irish, perhaps?

"Who—who are you?"

"I've brought a message from Caroline," he replied, and stepped forward, putting her gently to one side; then he closed the door, taking complete control of the situation. "I should not call anyone else, Mrs Kane. I want to talk to you alone," he went on quietly. "If you do what I tell you, Caroline will be all right."

Eve exclaimed: "Where is she?"

"We will come to that later."

"Don't be ridiculous! Where is my daughter?"

"Easy, now, easy," said the man, and took her right

wrist firmly. "Rollison may have gone out, but he has a servant, hasn't he?"

It was on the tip of her tongue to say that Jolly was ill, but she stopped herself.

The man repeated: "Hasn't he?" and when she didn't answer, he twisted her wrist—not enough to hurt but enough to show that he could hurt badly. "You must co-operate, Mrs Kane, or I can't make any promises about your daughter."

Eve said: "I want to know where she is."

"All you have to worry about is that she is quite all right, and will continue to be provided you do what you're told," the man said. "Where is this servant?"

Eve said, helplessly: "He—he's ill in bed."

"Well, how convenient!" the man exclaimed delightedly. "I told my brother this venture had all the signs of a lucky break. Where is he?" He urged her forward. "Take me round the flat. I like to be sure that I'm being told the truth."

She went round with him. He peeped into Jolly's room, and closed the door very softly, as if he were genuinely anxious not to disturb the sick man. Then they went back to the big room, and the man glanced at the Trophy Wall, and smiled rather one-sidedly, as if he were beginning to appreciate exactly what the trophies meant.

"I've read about Rollison, but I didn't realise he was quite such a personality," he said. "I hope you know that he's had failures as well as successes."

"What—what do you mean?"

"It is easy to chalk up the wins," remarked the sallow man, "but it is harder to point out that many of the murderers he eventually caught had killed several people before being stopped. It would not help you much to know that he managed to catch me, if Caroline were dead, would it?"

Eve said: "I think it's time you stopped trying to frighten me."

"*Trying*," the man echoed, and actually laughed and spread his hands; the nails were beautifully manicured, his suit was perfectly tailored. "I've never seen anyone more frightened than you are. And I don't blame you! But there's no need to be, provided you do exactly what you're told. Did Rollison tell you how much I want?"

"No."

"Then I'll tell you—twenty thousand pounds. That's not a lot of money to you, is it, Mrs Kane?" When she didn't answer, he went on: "Isn't Caroline worth that to you?"

She still didn't answer.

The doctor would be here at any moment; when he came, what should she do? She could tell him the truth, could make him send for the police, but—what would happen to Caroline if she did? All reason made her want to refuse to pay ransom, made her long to defy this man, but—*what would happen to Caroline?* He talked about his brother; he knew that Rolly had gone out, so that meant that he had been watching the flat. He gave an impression of complete self-confidence, as if he knew exactly what he was doing, and would carry out any threat he made.

He put his hand into his inside pocket, and drew something out, very slowly; suddenly she realised that it was another lock of Caroline's hair. She almost broke down at sight of it. She wanted to snatch it from him, wanted to shout and rave, but she knew that if she did she would have surrendered completely. She must not do that yet, somehow she must fight. He held the lock up in the air. The morning light gave it a lighter shade of auburn than the electric light had done last night. It was tied at one end with a piece of bright red ribbon—ribbon she had bought because one of the school rules was that all girls' hair should be tied back with ribbon, or plaited. He swung it to and fro, gently. It was nearly a foot long, and that meant it had been cut off close to the scalp. They might have hurt Caroline, cutting it off. Oh, God, what could she do to help Caroline?

"Would you like it, as a little memento?" the man inquired.

"No!"

"Perhaps Rollison would—suppose we start another wall for him," the man suggested, and sauntered across to the fireplace wall, where the portrait of an elderly man was hanging; these were miniatures, one of a man and one of a woman, on either side. He draped the lock of hair over one of the miniatures, turned to Eve and gave his wide smile, and said: "That is the wall where he puts the souvenirs of his failures, shall we say."

Eve could not stand this any longer, and she shouted: *"Where—where is Caroline?"*

"You can have her back, quite unharmed except for the loss of a little hair, in exchange for twenty thousand pounds and an assurance—which I shall work out—that you will not tell the police and will not allow Rollison to be present at the exchange."

"How do I know you would give Caroline back to me?"

"You don't, do you?" the man replied smoothly. "You have to take my word for it—just as I have to take your word that you won't have the police or Rollison with you. Or anyone. It's a simple bargain. But this may make you feel better: we don't want Caroline much longer. She'd only be a burden. So it's obviously very likely that we'll do what we promise."

Eve didn't answer—and while she was staring at him, hating the way he smiled, hating the smooth way he talked, and fighting her awful fears, there was another ring at the front door bell.

On the instant, the man moved forward and took her wrists, thrust his face close to hers and demanded:

"Who is it? Do you know?"

"It—it's the doctor, I expect. I—I sent for him." She

could no more lie to him than she could refuse to pay for Caroline. "Jolly is very ill. He—"

"The doctor can see Jolly, but don't you say a word about me. Understand? Don't say a word about who I am. Not a word. The knife that cut your daughter's hair could just as easily cut her throat," the man said.

12

THE BROTHERS

Dr Welling stood at the front door. He was a smaller man than Rollison, but not so short as the man in the living-room. He was middle-aged, had a brisk manner, and eyes which obviously missed very little. He stepped inside as Eve drew back, and said:

"I don't think we've met?"

"No, we haven't. I'm—Mrs Kane." Before she could add that she was a friend of Rollison, Welling said:

"You don't look exactly on top of the world yourself, Mrs Kane. Are you all right?"

"I—I've a severe headache."

"Hmm," said Welling. "I think Mr Rollison's the best doctor for your kind of headache! Assuming that you've brought a problem to him, you couldn't have come to a better man. Now, shall I go into Jolly? I know my way."

"Yes—please."

Dr Welling went the longer way round, and not into the living-room; it was almost as if he knew that she did not want him to go in there. Eve hesitated, then went back into the big room. The kidnapper was standing with his back to her, studying the Trophy Wall again, but the moment she appeared, he glanced round; and he whispered:

"You're doing all right."

She crossed to him swiftly.

"Please," she begged, "where is my daughter?"

"Quite safe."

"I must know where she is."

"It will cost you twenty thousand pounds."

"I don't care what it costs!"

"Are you sure about that?" the man asked, and his eyes lit up. "You know what you're saying?"

"Yes."

"Twenty—thousand—pounds."

"I can get it in an hour!"

"Yes, I know you can," replied the sallow-faced man. "You could get a lot more than that, too, but we aren't thinking of more, are we?" He paused for a moment, and then went on: "Rollison will try to stop you."

"I won't let him."

"Sure?"

"Yes! Don't keep wasting time."

"All right, Mrs Kane," the man said. "You get twenty thousand pounds in used one pound and five pound notes, and have it ready by—shall we say one o'clock? That will give you two hours. I will telephone you with instructions, and when I meet you, I will exchange Caroline for the money. Is that clearly understood?"

"Yes," she made herself say.

The man patted her hand, and said: "You're being very sensible. Don't let anyone make you change your mind. Now here are one or two details. The money must be in four separate parcels. Each must be wrapped in brown paper and tied round with red string or tape. Is that clear?"

"Yes, it's quite clear," Eve said, and clenched her hands as she went on: "You will hand Caroline over in exchange, won't you?"

"That's a promise," the man assured her. "You needn't have any fears, provided the police aren't told and Rollison isn't told." He took her hands again, tightly, with a threat of pain. "You should get out of here, you know. Rollison has quite a personality, and he might—"

"He won't make me change my mind! No one will."

"You must take the risk and remember that your daughter means more to you than twenty thousand pounds

D

does to me," the man said. "You aren't going to take my
telephone message here, though. If Rollison doesn't know
what I've told you to do, he can't interfere, and it will be
far safer if you do it my way." He took a white card from
his pocket, and held it in those beautifully kept fingers.
"Be at this telephone kiosk at half-past one. It's in the
foyer of the Astor Hotel, near Piccadilly, just round the
corner from the reception desk. You can't miss it, and
the number is on this card, to make sure you don't. I'll
telephone you there. Is that all quite clear?"

"Yes," Eve said, tautly.

"Don't forget that, if you do exactly what I tell you,
there'll be no bother, but if anyone follows you there'll
be such trouble for Caroline that you'll hate yourself for
the rest of your days. How old is she?"

"Sixteen."

"As they say, just awakening to womanhood," the man
said gently. "We don't want it to be a rude awakening,
do we?"

Horror welled up in Eve.

"Oh, God! You wouldn't do—"

"We won't hurt Caroline in any way provided you do
exactly what I tell you," the man promised her. "Half-
past one, at that number."

He smiled, squeezed her hand, and turned away.

She wanted to rush after him, she wanted to beg and
plead with him, she wanted some definite assurance that
Caroline was all right, and would not be harmed. She did
not move. The man's back was very broad—absurdly
broad—and his trousers were very narrow. He wore light
brown suede shoes; in a way, he was a dandy. He went
into the lounge hall without looking back; and as he
disappeared, Eve found herself impelled to run after him,
to stand in the doorway, and cry:

"Swear to me that she will be all right."

He turned and faced her, and said solemnly: "I swear
to you that she will not be hurt if you do what I say." He

opened the front door and went out. She did not notice that he had no difficulty with the lock at the door. She heard it close. She leaned against the wall of the lounge hall without realising what she was doing. She heard movements in the flat, and remembered Dr Welling: she had completely forgotten him, even forgotten him when she had called out. He might have heard her. She turned round in alarm, and saw him entering the big room. He looked grave, glanced at her, then stepped to the telephone and lifted it. He dialled a number, looked at her again, and frowned.

"Do you know when Mr Rollison will be back?"

"Fairly—fairly soon, I think."

"Will you be here until he comes?"

"Yes, if—if he isn't too late."

"Ask him to telephone me as soon as he gets in, will you?" Welling said, and then broke off. "Excuse me . . . Hallo, Bridie—Bridie, I'm not happy about Rollison's man Jolly, not a bit happy. He's running a hundred and three, and it might be peritonitis. Lay on the ambulance and have a bed ready, will you? . . . 22 Gresham Terrace, that's right . . . Twenty minutes will do." He rang off, and looked straight at Eve, but this time he hardly seemed to notice her. "Rollison is devoted to Jolly. If anything should happen to him—"

He went on talking.

It hardly made sense to Eve, but a kind of sense emerged; that Rolly would be desperately concerned for his man, that he would not be able to concentrate on helping her, that she was on her own; utterly on her own.

". . . and now I want a look at you," Dr Welling said, and came towards her.

"No! I'm all right."

"Don't be silly," Welling said. "You're anything but all right. How bad is the situation?"

"It's—it's very bad."

"Is Rollison working on it?"

"Yes."

"That man can work miracles," Welling said. "Now, I wonder if you can get some blankets, and ..."

. . . .

Eve watched the ambulance men take Jolly out. She saw his grey face, and realised how right the doctor was to be worried about him. She closed the door on Dr Welling, who did not waste words on further attempts at reassurance. At least she had been busy for the last half an hour. Now she was really on her own, and she knew exactly what she had to do. She was quite sure that Rollison would try to dissuade her. He would have plenty on his mind, too; far too much.

She hated to run away from him, but must leave before he came back.

That decision had hardly been reached before she began to move, half-running round the flat. She kept glancing out of the window, but there was no sign of Rollison or his car; only a few people were in the street. She could telephone him about Jolly. It would be a shock when he came back and found Jolly gone, but she could telephone in half an hour; he was bound to be back by then.

He might have found out where Caroline was!

The thought seemed to affect her like a physical blow. She stood unmoving, staring in front of her towards the door leading to the domestic quarters. She thought of everything that Rollison had done; how he had said immediately that he would drive her down to Hapley; how he had tried with the police, used his influence with Scotland Yard; gone off this morning after only a few hours' sleep; been ready to drop everything else for her. There was more, too: the way he affected her, the fact that she felt so completely at home with him.

How could she walk out on such a man?

But he would want her to ignore the man's orders, and would fight against paying the ransom money.

How did she know?

He might say that it would be wise to pay it; he might say that the first task was to get Caroline safe and, when that was done, go for the men who had kidnapped her and try to get the money back. Dr Welling had said that he could work miracles; she could believe it. His calmness and his common sense must impress anyone. He was an expert, even Scotland Yard acknowledged it. How *could* she walk out on him now?

If it were a question of walking out on him, or taking great risks with Caroline, there was no question of what she should do. She remembered the way the man had talked about Caroline awakening to womanhood. She shivered. Only Caroline mattered, and what Rollison thought or felt about her, Eve, was unimportant. She had to decide which way she could best help Caroline— with Rollison's help, or without it?

She had on her hat and gloves, all ready to go out; she could close the door on everything this flat meant to her. She could go and see her bank manager, arrange for the money to be packed in four parcels, could do exactly what she liked, but if she did the wrong thing, then it might mean horror and death for Caroline.

She said aloud: "He can't stop me from paying!"

She thought: 'I can't walk out now. I've got to tell him about Jolly, and tell him what I'm going to do. I'll have to stay.'

But he might find a way of stopping her, if he really thought that paying the money was the wrong thing to do.

She must not stand here vacillating! She must decide—

The telephone bell rang, startling her. She turned round in the big room and stared at the telephone. From this angle it was immediately beneath the hangman's noose, that macabre evidence of Rollison's expertness. The bell had a mellow ring, but as it went on and on she hated the sound. Then she told herself that it might be Rollison. She might be able to tell him what had happened and what she was going to do, and leave without feeling that she had betrayed him in any way. She went across and picked up the telephone.

"Hallo."

A man said: "Is that Mrs Kane?"

"Speaking."

"Mrs Kane, I have a very important message for Rollison," the man said, and now she recognised the voice, with its slight accent; a hated voice and a hated, smiling face. "He is on his way home, and has my brother with him. I want you to tell him that unless he releases my brother immediately—and I mean immediately, not in half an hour's time—then nothing will save your daughter. Tell Rollison exactly what I say."

He rang off.

She felt a more awful fear than ever before.

One decision had been made for her; she had to stay. But if Rollison had caught this man's brother, if he could so alarm the other man that he could make him give this warning, what else could Rollison do? The awful indecision was even worse. She had never known seconds drag as they did; the hands of her wrist-watch hardly seemed to go round at all. She kept going to the window and looking out; and as she turned away, ten minutes or so after the call had been made, she saw the pearl-grey Rolls-Bentley turn the corner. She pressed her face against the window to make sure; she could not see Rollison or a passenger, but when the car stopped Rollison jumped out on the far side, came round, unlocked the near side door, and stood aside for a man to step out.

For a moment she felt almost wild with relief, for she thought it was the man who had called on her. He had broad shoulders, he had black hair, he was short, he had narrow trousers . . . and then she saw that he had leather shoes, not the light brown suede. She saw, too, that he was smaller than the man who had been here. She was losing her mind—this was the brother.

Rollison looked up, saw her, waved, grinned broadly, and pointed at the man with him, a man whose wrist he held as if determined not to let him go. Then, they disappeared.

Rollison was coming back in triumph, not dreaming what lay in store for him.

13

STALEMATE

ROLLISON saw Eve at the window, waved, and pushed Max towards the front door, holding his arm behind him. If the man were going to make an attempt to escape, it would be now. There were several people in the street, and Rollison kept close to the other, so that no one should see the grip that he had on his wrist. He was prepared for a swift back-heel, but there was no pause in Max's movements. He seemed completely subdued—until they reached the porch of the house.

He back-heeled viciously.

Rollison first felt the tension at his arms, guessed what was coming, let him go and skipped to one side. Then, he pushed him in the small of the back. Max, taken completely by surprise, staggered forward against the front door; it boomed. Rollison thrust a key in the lock, turned the handle and pushed the door open, pushed again and, by the time Max regained his balance, they were standing inside the hall with the door closed.

"You left it too late," he remarked.

There was no smile on Max's face now, only a look of viciousness.

"You'll suffer for this, Rollison,"

"Don't disappoint me," Rollison pleaded. "So far it's been refreshing to talk to you, you haven't the customary thug's spiel. Go straight up to the top floor."

Max turned and went ahead of him. If he were going to make another attempt to get free it would almost certainly be at one of the landings. He made none. Soon they were at the door of Rollison's flat. Had Jolly been well, he would have been at the open door by now, and Rollison had half expected Eve to be. He was disappointed that she wasn't, but the disappointment faded when he heard a sound on the other side of the door, and a moment later, the door opened.

He smiled at her, absurdly pleased to display his prisoner. Then he saw her expression, and on that instance all the pleasure and satisfaction dropped away. She looked terribly distressed. Her face had no colour at all, and her wide set eyes were shadowed as if with great fear. He shouldn't have left her alone. He saw her step back; and he saw the way Max glanced at her, as if he knew that this woman would give very little trouble.

Max said: "What's the matter? Do you miss your darling daughter?"

Eve winced.

Rollison felt a surge of anger, greater than the moment warranted, caused almost entirely by the fact that the man had hurt Eve. He dropped a hand to Max's shoulder, spun him round, and then slapped him across the face, once, twice, thrice. Max backed away, hands up trying to defend himself, eyes glinting with fear. Rollison spoke as savagely as he had acted.

"Don't be so clever again." He closed the door, and it clicked sharply. "Eve, what's the matter?"

"I—I must see you alone," she said.

Max was standing, sullen, and red-faced where Rollison had struck him, near the door leading to the living-room. Usually Jolly would be on call, and would look after the man; but as far as Rollison knew, Jolly was in his bedroom. There was no doubt that Eve meant exactly what she said; so there had been fresh trouble.

He turned to Max.

"This way, and look slippy." His tone made the man obey; and now Max seemed to have recovered, for he was smiling a little, and his body was less tense. "Straight ahead," Rollison ordered, and Max went into the passage

D*

leading to the back of the flat. "First door on the left," he ordered again after a moment; it was the lavatory. "Get inside." He took the key out of the inside of the door and, when Max went in, put it on the outside.

"Rollison," Max said, "don't forget that you're taking a lot of risks with that Kane girl, will you? How would you like to have her on your conscience?" The words were very clearly uttered, and obviously meant to carry to Eve.

Rollison made no comment, closed and locked the door, and turned round. Eve was standing near the end of the passage, and she must have heard. She looked—ill. Rollison felt an overwhelming desire to help, to comfort and to reassure her. He wanted to put his arms round her, and lead her into the big room, and tell her that there was not a thing to worry about; but words would be empty.

"What is it?" he asked quietly.

"I've had—a visitor," she said, and then told him in a husky voice, obviously making a great effort to be dispassionate. "This—this man's brother. He says . . ."

Listening and watching, Rollison knew that this was not everything. He knew something else; he would have to let Max go. There were moments to fight and moments to be refused to be pushed, but this was not one of either. At least Eve had kept her head well enough to make sure that Max did not know the position yet; it might be possible to get more out of Max.

When she had finished, he asked: "What else, Eve?"

"Rolly," she said, and hesitated, and then burst out: "I can't help it, I've got to get Caroline back! I've got to pay the ransom."

He didn't speak.

"Don't you understand, I've got to," Eve said, desperately. "I can't help what happens after that. If you'd talked to that man, if you'd heard what he said, what he threatened to do to Caroline if I didn't pay the money, you would know what I mean. I've got to pay him."

"Keep your voice low," Rollison said, and led her across the room to his desk. "Sit down, Eve, and—"

"I can't keep still." She moved towards the window, and stood for a moment with her back to it. "I know what you'll say, but I can't help it. I've got to pay."

"Twenty thousand pounds . . ."

"Twenty, forty, sixty, I don't care how much it costs, I've got to get Caroline back," Eve cried. "I'm terribly sorry, I should never have come to you. I've wasted your time. I must save Caroline."

Rollison said: "Supposing they take the money and then ask for more?"

It was as if he had slapped her.

"They won't do that!"

"It's been done before."

"You're only saying it because you don't want me to pay the ransom, because it would mean that you'd lost a case. You have lost cases, haven't you? People who have come to you for help *have* died, haven't they?"

Very slowly, Rollison admitted: "Yes." He knew that it would be useless to reason with her; whatever else he had to do, it would be on his own. She might be right, too. Max had insisted that all they wanted was twenty thousand pounds, and this might be one of the cases where it would be a fair exchange; if 'fair' was the word. "Listen, Eve," he went on, "the important thing is to get Caroline back. If you think the only way is to pay the ransom, then you'll have to pay it. I want to make sure that it's not wasted, that's all."

"There isn't anything you can do," Eve insisted. "I— I'm terribly sorry, but—this man said that I wasn't to tell you anything about how I was to pay the money, how he was to get in touch with me. I have to handle this by myself. And you—you've plenty to worry about without me, anyhow."

He didn't understand that remark.

"Eve, all I want to do is help you. Surely you know that." He never meant it more deeply.

"Then let that man go, and let me go," Eve said. "It's the only way."

"We could make a fatal mistake," he warned her. "They have Caroline, and the way this man talked to you proves how much he wants to make sure his brother isn't hurt. An exchange of the brother for Caroline—"

"I daren't risk it," Eve said, almost shrill with desperation. "You can't possibly understand, Rolly. You haven't any children of your own. Caroline is part of me. She's part of my life. If anything like this were to happen to her, it would send me mad. Don't you understand what he threatened to do?"

"Yes," said Rollison. "I understand it perfectly. I still think that I could handle this situation better than you. No, don't interrupt. I could send this brother out with a message: that I'll act for you, I'll take the twenty thousand pounds, I'll hand it over in exchange for Caroline. He's less likely to cheat me."

"*What makes you so sure that he'll cheat me?*" she cried.

Rollison looked at her for a long time, and then said very quietly:

"All right, Eve. You must do what you think best. I'll go and get Max." He left her alone, seeing the way her hands fell by her side and her expression changed, as if now that she had her own way, she wondered whether it was wise. She did not move. He unlocked the door on Max, and Max stepped out, smiling tautly, obviously determined to demonstrate his self-control. "Go the way you came," Rollison ordered, "and don't try to run." They reached the big room, where Eve was standing with her handbag and her gloves in hand, ready to go; and Max looked astonished but delighted. "Max," Rollison said, "your brother has been here."

"I wondered when you'd find out about Felix," Max said.

"Felix has come to terms with Mrs Kane," Rollison went on. "The exchange of her daughter for twenty thousand pounds." The deliberate way in which he spoke seemed to worry Max, and stop him from smiling so broadly. "That's how it's to be. An exchange. Don't double-cross Mrs Kane. Make sure that Caroline isn't hurt. I want Mrs Kane and her daughter back here by six o'clock this evening. If they're not—"

Max said swiftly: "Rollison, they will be!" His eyes were glistening, and he looked as if he were really delighted. "Felix and I won't double-cross anyone; twenty thousand pounds is all we asked for and all we want. You've got more good sense than I expected!" He was trying to restrain his excitement. "Did Felix fix the details?"

"With Mrs Kane."

"That's the way it should be," Max enthused. "Rollison, so long as you don't try to follow, so long as you don't warn the police, that girl will be delivered safe and sound."

"I can't prevent the police from working it out for themselves," Rollison said.

Max gave his broadest, brightest smile.

"If you really want to help Mrs Kane, I'd find a way of preventing them," he said.

"Yes."

"So this is the great Toff," marvelled Max. "He doesn't even fight."

"I don't fight at the cost of the life of a girl of sixteen."

"That's your trouble, you're too much of a gentleman," Max said, but it wasn't really a sneer. "Mrs Kane, remind me to tell you about the way he turned his back on—" He stopped abruptly, did not mention the name Leah, and then went to the door; he had an air of incredulity, as if he could not really believe that he was going to walk out. He reached the door leading to the lounge hall, and Rollison called:

"Max.'

"Well?" Max turned his head.

"Six o'clock this evening, unhurt."

"Only a few hairs of her head," Max said. He put a hand to his forehead and flicked a salute, then went to the front door; Rollison heard it open and close. He did not go towards it, but stood looking at Eve, trying not to show what he felt, knowing that she was anxious to say something else, hoping that she would not.

"I think it was worth taking the chance," he said. "If not, then we'll try again. Are you sure you can get the money?"

"Yes," she declared, almost breathlessly. "I can go and see my bank manager at once, he's very near—at Dover Court," she added, not realising that he knew that there was only one bank in that tiny square off Piccadilly.

"And we'll take this off until the show's really over." He removed the lock of hair, and put it on his desk.

He did not tell Eve that the moment she went out he would be at the telephone, talking to an old friend in the East End, making sure that at least two men were ready to follow her to her bank when she got the cash. If she suspected that for a moment, she would find some other way of getting the twenty thousand pounds.

"You've been—wonderful," she said. She stepped forward swiftly, took his hands, and kissed him full on the lips. There was a sheen of tears in her eyes. "I'll never forget you." She turned away and reached the door, and he wished she would go quickly, hoped she would not speak again; but suddenly she turned round, and now there was a different expression in her eyes: a kind of alarm.

"Rolly!" she exclaimed. "I didn't tell you—"

"Forget it, Eve."

"It's Jolly! Dr Welling has sent him to hospital. He thinks there may have to be an emergency operation."

Rollison drew in a sharp breath.

"Where is he?"

"The Central London Hospital."

"Thanks," Rollison said slowly. "Thanks, Eve." For the first time he felt glad that he would not have to follow her himself; for the first time he forgot her, her Caroline and her husband, in this new, frightening anxiety. Caroline was part of her life; in a different way, Jolly was part of his. "Eve—"

"Yes?"

"If there's anything you want, now or at any time, come and see me."

"I will," she promised huskily.

He went after her to the door, but she had opened it and was outside before he reached it, and she did not look round. He waited until she was at the first landing, then swung round and almost ran into the living-room, snatched up the receiver, and dialled the Whitechapel number. The ringing sound went on and on, and every moment was an agony of waiting. He kept seeing Jolly's face in his mind's eye.

The ringing sound stopped.

"Ebbutt's Gym," a man with a wheezy voice answered.

"Bill," said Rollison, "I haven't a second to waste. Listen . . ."

He described Eve and the clothes she was wearing; he described Max; and he gave the address of the Midpro Bank in Dover Court.

"I've got that—I'll fix it," Ebbutt promised. "Mustn't let the woman out of our sight—that right?"

"Send two men and watch the woman and anyone with her," Rollison urged. "Thanks, Bill, I'll be ringing you." He rang off, then dialled Dr Welling's number, feeling a sense of guilt for having put Eve before Jolly even for a few minutes.

Almost at once a woman answered: "Welling's receptionist. Dr Welling's surgery."

"Bridie, how's Jolly?" Rollison's heart thumped painfully.

"Oh, I'm so glad you've called, Mr Rollison," the receptionist said. "Dr Welling's at the hospital now, and they are operating at once. It was a burst appendix. There's always a *very* good chance even with the elderly, but the doctor thinks it would be better if you were at the hospital, just in case."

Rollison thought: 'It's almost as if this was the way it was meant to be.' He said: "I'll go straight away, Bridie." He hesitated, and then added, "Central London?"

"Yes."

"Thanks," said Rollison.

He hurried out. The Rolls-Bentley was standing pointing in the direction of the hospital in Westminster. He was getting into the driving seat when a car turned the corner, and on the instant he recognised a car from Scotland Yard; as they passed he recognised a Chief Inspector who was certainly on the way to see him. He pretended not to notice the man, reached the corner, and swung round.

At the corner he saw Max, sitting at the wheel of a small M.G. sports car, painted dark green. Max actually grinned and waved, then started off. The little car roared and the big purred its way across the West End, until Rollison turned into the courtyard of the hospital. Max drove past the entrance, with a final wave.

Rollison thought: 'Bill, don't lose her,' and pulled up where there was just room to park, and hurried to the entrance. As he stepped through he saw Dr Welling and, in that moment, Eve Kane was completely forgotten.

"Jolly's still in the theatre," Welling announced.

14

£20,000

THE bank manager was a younger man than his grey hair suggested, tall, very affable, more than a little anxious. He had given the instructions for the money to be obtained and packed in four packets of equal size and value, and now Eve sat in front of his desk, while he drew at a cigarette, twiddled his hands, and said yet again:

"You do understand that this is most unusual, Mrs Kane, don't you?"

"Yes."

"I'm not sure that it is wise for you to have a large sum of money like that with you."

"I shan't have it for long."

"Would you mind telling me what you intend to buy with it?" asked the manager. He gave a rather harassed little smile. "I can't imagine any ordinary—any normal—thing for which your cheque wouldn't be good enough."

"This time, I need cash."

"Yes, of course," He squashed out his cigarette, and then asked: "How is Mr Kane?"

"Very well, thank you."

"Good. I'm very glad to hear it," said the manager over-heartily. "Very glad. I—ah, here it is." There was a tap at the door, and two men came in, each carrying two parcels. One could have carried the four, but not with comfort. "Can I—er—can I send a messenger with you?" That struck him as a brilliant idea. "I will, gladly! Richards—"

"No, thank you," Eve said. "I've brought this case." She had stopped on the way and bought a lightweight fibre case, but now she wondered whether it would be large enough; the physical difficulty of handling so much money had not occurred to her before. "And I have a taxi waiting."

"I'd be happier—"

"Mr Gray, will you please give me the credit for knowing exactly what I am doing," Eve said sharply.

Gray looked first startled, then offended. "Oh. Yes, very well, Mrs Kane." He stood aside while the two men put the money into the case, then pressed it and closed the lid; it just fastened. One of the men picked it up, and pulled a face.

"It's rather heavy, sir."

"Take the case to the taxi for Mrs Kane," ordered the manager coldly. "Good afternoon, Mrs Kane."

"Good afternoon," Eve said.

From the way the case was carried, making the man lean to one side, and from the way in which it was pushed along the floor of the taxi, it must be heavy. She wondered how she would manage to carry it when she reached the Astor Hotel. The porter would take it for her, of course, there would be no trouble actually at the hotel, but afterwards the problem might become really difficult. She sat back, her eyes smarting, wishing she had not snapped at the bank manager for doing his job. She kept thinking of the way Rollison had looked at her when she had finally made him understand that she was going to have her own way. If Rollison were with her, there would be no problem about carrying the money. She stared at the case, oblivious to the traffic, until the taxi pulled up outside the Astor Hotel. Parked close to the entrance was an M.G. sports car. A porter came up, and Eve saw Max standing near the revolving doors, smiling, nodding approval. She also saw, although without noticing, a man on a motor scooter and another in a small, very old car, drawing up just behind her; she had not noticed them near the bank, either.

The porter opened the door, took out the case, but did not find it too difficult to carry.

"Are you staying—" he began.

Then Max came up, hand outstretched, beaming.

"Hallo, there, you're dead on time," he greeted. "All right, porter, we're taking the case to the baggage room." He slipped half a crown into the porter's hand, took Eve's arm, and followed the case without speaking; the baggage room was at one side of the entrance hall, with a diminutive man in charge. "Hold this for an hour or two, will you?" asked Max, and another half-crown changed hands, as he went on: "You'll give me a ticket, won't you —thank you." He took a ticket, gave it to Eve, and watched her put it in her handbag. "Come on, we'll be late," he said to Eve, and took her away from the baggage room and across the little foyer of the second-class hotel. From the moment he had appeared, he had taken complete charge of the situation. "We'll go out the other way," he said, and she saw a passage leading to a side door and a street which she did not know. "There's a nice little restaurant across the road, and I've reserved a table."

"I don't—" she began.

"You've got to eat and so have I, and we might as well eat together," Max said. "You've got the receipt for the case; there's nothing at all to worry about. After lunch, Caroline will be here."

Eve's heart leapt.

"Here?"

"She'll be in the hotel foyer, I promise you."

Eve said: "She must be." She felt a frightening uncertainty which had not been there before. It was all too easy. The man seemed remarkably open and frank, but— he *had* kidnapped Caroline—he *had* run down that policeman. He or his brother had, anyhow. She had almost forgotten that. These men were hardened criminals, and she'd known that Max's brother had meant what he said when he'd threatened Caroline. Oh, God, why had she come on her own? Why hadn't she allowed Rollison to handle the situation? All that money was in the baggage room, and the little ticket in her handbag meant practically nothing at all. She allowed Max to lead her into a small restaurant, one of the coffee-bar kind which had a small room for main meals. Their table was in a corner, close to the window.

"It's not licensed here, but I'm sure you won't mind that," said Max. He picked up a plastic menu, and handed it to her. "What will you have?"

"I—I really don't feel that I can eat."

"Oh, nonsense!" He looked at the card. "Have something light—the omelettes here are very good. I can tell you that from past experience."

"All right."

"A mushroom omelette, perhaps? Or *fines herbes*?"

"I really don't mind."

"You're worrying too much," Max chided, and leaned forward and squeezed her hand. "You needn't, my dear. In an hour we'll go across there, and you'll see Caroline actually in the hotel lobby. My brother will be with her. As soon as I have the case, he'll leave her by herself. She'll feel a little strange—she has slept a lot—and her memory may be a little shaky, but by tomorrow she'll be absolutely herself again. There isn't a thing to worry about."

Please God, let that be the truth, Eve prayed.

The omelette was large, and served with crispy fried chips; she was surprised not only that she could eat but enjoy it. She did not want anything else, but Max, opposite her, and attentive as Rollison would have been, followed a steak with cheese and biscuits; she noticed that his nails were beautifully manicured, like his brother's, and that he was just as immaculate. She wondered what made men who could behave like this turn bad.

Then, she yawned.

It wasn't surprising; she hadn't slept more than three hours the previous night, little the night before. She stifled another yawn.

"Will you take coffee?" asked the waitress.

"Yes—black or white, Eve?" asked Max.

"Black, please." Black coffee would help her to keep awake. It was ridiculous to feel so sleepy now, when, if he had told the truth, she would be seeing Caroline within half an hour. *Half an hour!* She could not bring herself to believe that this man had lied to her; he seemed so truthful, so pleasant now that he had his own way. And, for Caroline, twenty thousand pounds was nothing at all. Not long ago she had hated her wealth, because that was what had tied Ralph to her; now almost for the first time she really felt thankful for it. She tried to feel excited, tried to induce a sense of exhilaration, but the truth was she was absolutely exhausted. It must be the reaction after the excitement. Her eyes felt heavy, and all she wanted to do was to lean her head against the wall behind her, and doze for a few minutes.

Why shouldn't she?

It was ridiculous; she must not! That black coffee would be here in a moment.

"Sugar?" Max asked, and spooned white sugar into the coffee when it arrived. She stirred and sipped it, and within five minutes her head nodded. She saw Max smiling his broad, beaming smile at her, and she knew that she could not keep awake. The sight of his smile and the glint of triumph in his eyes was the first real warning she had that this was no longer natural tiredness, that somehow he had managed to drug her.

He had put the sugar in her coffee!

I mustn't lose consciousness, she thought desperately; but her eyes were closing, even her fears were sluggish, and she leaned forward, chin on her breast, unconscious.

Max beamed at her . . .

"She's had a long journey, travelled most of the night,"

Max told the waitress. "May I leave her here for twenty minutes or so? I've a couple of telephone calls to make, and it seems a shame to wake her."

"She'll be all right there," the waitress assured him.

Max stood up, hesitated, then quite openly picked up Eve's handbag, unfastened it, and made a lot of jingling noise taking out small change as if for the telephone; doing so, he palmed the ticket for the suitcase. He closed the bag, put it close to Eve's side, and went to the cash desk. He looked across at Eve from the window outside, and grinned as he stepped into the side entrance of the hotel. Two minutes later, he exchanged the ticket for the case. He carried it out to the M.G., dumped it in the back, and saw his brother standing near the hotel. He gave the thumbs up sign, and drove off; and his brother waved for a taxi.

. . . .

"She's absolute dead asleep," the waitress said to the manageress of the little restaurant. "The man with her said he was going to make some telephone calls, but that's an hour ago. What shall I do?"

"Well, she isn't in the way there, and she might as well get her sleep in," the manageress said. "She looks very tired. Did he pay?"

"Oh, yes."

"Well, you go off, and don't forget to be back at four o'clock sharp. We've that party of Swedes coming for the *smorgasbord*. I'll keep an eye on her."

Eve slept . . .

"I really think we'll have to wake her," the manageress said, uneasily, a little before four o'clock. "I hope she's all right. She—she couldn't be *dead*, could she?"

"Good heavens!" the afternoon waitress gasped. "That would be a do, wouldn't it?" They approached Eve, and then the girl said: "No, she's breathing, you can see her breast rising and falling. Thank Gawd for that." She watched the manageress step up to Eve, and touch her shoulder—

Eve felt the touch.

She had been rising to the surface of consciousness for some time, aware of noises, of moments of quietness, of voices, of cars passing in the street, and of footsteps; but she had not really thought about those things, and had not realised where she was. Then she felt someone shaking her and tried to open her eyes, but they were so heavy. She heard a woman saying:

"Wake up, madam, please. *Please* wake up."

At last her eyes opened, and almost at once she realised where she was, and that she was alone.

.   .   .   .

The ticket and the case had gone, and there was no sign of Caroline, no hope of seeing Caroline. There was only horror in Eve's mind.

15

REPORT

"I should say there is more than a fifty-fifty chance now," said Welling. "In fact I'm sure there is, Rollison. I will make sure that Jolly gets everything he needs; you can forget about him. If there's the slightest sign of a change for the worse, I'll tell you—and you can contact my surgery or my flat any time you like to pick up a message. It won't do you any harm to be busy. Most attractive woman at your flat, although I've seldom seen anyone looking more tired. My strong advice is that you find some way to make her rest."

"Ah, yes," said Rollison. "Thanks." He smiled, although he did not feel at all like smiling and was not sure whether to believe Welling about Jolly: the doctor might simply be trying to ease his mind. "Wouldn't it be better if I stayed at the hospital for a while?"

"Absolutely no point in it at all," answered Welling. "You've just seen him—and he'll be unconscious like that for at least twelve hours, probably for twenty-four. Take my advice, Rolly—go back and carry on with whatever job you're handling. And don't forget what I told you about Mrs Kane; she is very near collapse."

"Yes," Rollison said mechanically. "Thanks again."

He went across the courtyard of the hospital to the Rolls-Bentley. When he opened the door, heat came out as from a hot oven. He got in, wound down the window, and started off. It was nearly three o'clock; he had been at the hospital for three hours. He wondered where Eve was, and whether by any freak of chance she had Caroline back. Now that the worst of the emergency with Jolly was over, he could think more clearly about Eve. He should have put up a stronger fight, and would have done with nine people out of ten. Why hadn't he found some way of making her let him deal with Max and the brother, what was his name? Felix.

Max and Felix.

Supposing he had? He would have had to come to the hospital, anyhow, without being able to give his mind to the problem. As things had worked out, it had probably been wise to let Eve have her own way: if anything did go wrong this time, she wasn't likely to argue with him in future. He hoped desperately that it would not go wrong, as he drove as fast as the traffic would let him to Gresham Terrace. He hoped to see an old T model Ford outside, the car which Bill Ebbutt of the gymnasium drove with great pride; but it wasn't there. None of Ebbutt's men from the East End was in sight. Rollison went in and up the stairs. There had been times when he would have hesitated at the front door, wondering if all was well; but there was no reason for danger; as far as Max knew, he had given way.

Had Ebbutt's men got to the bank in time? Had they followed Eve?

He went in. The flat had a slightly woebegone look, oddments were out of place, a newspaper was on the floor of the lounge hall; none of these things would have been so had Jolly been at home; there was even a thin film of dust everywhere. Jolly would be away for at least four weeks, and possibly twice as long. It would be necessary to get someone in to take his place; one of Ebbutt's men had come before and would doubtless come again.

Rollison went to his desk and dialled Ebbutt's number, and again he had to wait a long time before it was answered. He felt hungry; he must have been hungry for a long time, but hadn't realised it. He could get a snack and—

"Ebbutt's Gym," Bill Ebbutt announced

"Rollison here, Bill."

"Oh, Mr Ar! Bin trying to get you on the phone," Ebbutt said quickly. "That right Jolly's been took ill?"

"He's just had a serious operation."

"Oh, Gawd," said Ebbutt. "He's not going to kick the bucket, Mr Ar, is he?"

"The doctor says not, Bill."

"Never can trust these perishing doctors; says what comes into their mind so as to stop you worrying," Ebbutt said roundly. "Mr Ar, I can imagine how you feel, I can really. Tell you what, though. Percy Wrightson's not working at the moment; he wouldn't say no to a chance to come over and help out. That be any use?"

"I'd be very glad, Bill. Thanks. Any news from those two men you sent to the Midpro Bank?"

"As a matter of fact, Mr Ar, there isn't," said Ebbutt. "I was wondering if you'd heard anyfink, as a matter of fact. I told them to report to you first; there wasn't any need to report to me unless they couldn't get hold of you. I sent Harry Mills and Joe Locket; couldn't do better if I tried. 'Eard nothink from either of them yet?"

"No."

"I'll call you the minute I hear, if they do ring up," promised Ebbutt, "and I'll send Percy over in time to get your dinner." He paused. "Okay, Mr Ar?"

"Thanks, Bill, that's fine," said Rollison.

He replaced the receiver and went into the kitchen. He saw the toaster in a different position from usual, bread still on the board, a tea tray with dirty cups and saucers. He went to the larder; at least that was well stocked, with ham, bread, butter and cheese. He opened a bottle of beer, made himself a good meal, and at ten minutes to four was standing all the dirty things on the draining board; Percy Wrightson could look after them when he came in.

Why wasn't there any word from Harry Mills and Joe Locket? They were middle-aged, able men, and had often helped Rollison when he had been working as the

Toff. He had heard Yard men say that those two, as well as others who worked for Ebbutt, would have made excellent detectives with a little more training, for they had a natural intelligence and quickness of eye and mind. Had Rollison himself been able to choose, he would have chosen the pair.

He went to the big room, hesitated, then turned up the number of the Midpro Bank at Dover Court; there was a chance that the manager hadn't left the office. The call was answered promptly, and in a moment the manager was on the line.

"Good afternoon, Mr Rollison! You may remember, we met once last year, when . . ." He was eager to make claim to acquaintanceship.

Rollison let him finish, and then said: "Yes, of course I remember." The manager was delighted. "Mr Gray, can you tell me if Mrs Kane has been in today, to take out a large sum of money?"

The manager hesitated, and then said in a much colder voice: "I'm sure you understand that I cannot betray a client's confidence, Mr Rollison." He sounded stuffy and pompous. "But—ah—yes, she has been here. Yes."

"Can you tell me what time she left?"

"At a little after twenty minutes to two."

"Was she alone?"

"Yes." The manager dragged that word out, and then went on much more briskly: "I am sure that it wouldn't be breaking a confidence to say that I was very worried about her, Mr Rollison. She looked ill—positively ill. And she was—well, perhaps I shouldn't say this, but she certainly wasn't herself. Do *you* know what she was planning to do with that very large—"

He broke off.

"Twenty thousand pounds," said Rollison quietly.

"So you know?"

"I know that she was going to make one or two large

purchases, and I wanted to make sure that she wasn't being swindled." Rollison said.

"You can't *imagine* what a relief that is to me," exclaimed the manager. "To feel that you are looking after her interests relieves me of all anxiety. I'm quite sure that . . ."

When Rollison rang off, he thought: 'So she didn't lose a minute.'

It was just after four o'clock. He wished even more fervently that there were some news from Harry or Joe. It would be pointless to telephone the hospital, but staying in and waiting was the last thing he wanted to do today. Yet if he went out, he might miss a message. He went to his desk and picked up the photograph of Eve, her husband and Caroline, which Eve had left for him. He did not look at the child or the man, only at Eve. He put it down slowly, frowned and said:

"What the devil is the matter with me? Why should she be so important?"

Was it really that his nerves were frayed because of Jolly?

The telephone bell rang. He picked up the receiver quickly, gave his number, and heard the pennies drop into a call box at the other end as someone pressed Button A. He was taut and tense as he stood up; then a Cockney voice came very clearly: it was Joe Locket.

"Mr Rollison there?"

"Hallo, Joe," Rollison greeted, and his heart was beginning to thump. "How've you been getting on?"

"Well, to tell you the truth, it's bin a funny turn up for the book," Joe declared. "We got to the bank as hinstructed, Mr Ar, no trouble about that, and abaht twenty minutes arterwards, out this dame comes—I mean, this lady showed up. She had a whacking great suitcase which one of the clurks carried for her, and a taxi was waiting."

Joe paused; one of his troubles was that he wanted to make absolutely sure that he omitted no details, and

Rollison knew from experience that he would lose the thread if he were interrupted.

"Yes," Rollison encouraged.

"Well, 'Arry followed 'er in 'is baby Orstin, I 'ad me Vespa," Joe went on. "We didn't 'ave no trouble abaht that, neever. Went to the Astor 'Otel, she did—you know it?"

"Yes, Joe."

"Awkward place, that Astor, 'cause there are two ways out," Joe explained. "So 'Arry stayed at the front entrance and I went rahnd to the back—just in case they went out that way."

"They?" asked Rollison quickly.

"Gorblimey, I'll forget me 'ead next," said Joe, in explosive self disgust. "There was a cove waiting for 'er—just like the bloke you described to Bill, Mr Ar. Be a Teddy boy if he wasn't too old. Greeted her like a long lorst friend, 'e did, and they went inside together."

"With the case?"

"Yes, they took that all right," answered Joe. "Well, I went rahnd the back, like I said, and a few minutes arterwards this lady and the bloke with her go into a little café, and . . ."

'Get on with it,' Rollison thought, but he forced himself to listen.

". . . when the bloke left I 'ad to make up me mind pretty damn quick whether to go arter 'im or whether to stay and look arter the lady, Mr Ar. Which would you have done?" Joe asked naïvely; and obviously he wanted to be quite sure that he had done the right thing.

"Watched her, Joe." Please God, he had.

"Strewth, that's a relief! That's the very thing I did," declared Joe. "The bloke went back into the Astor and never came aht no more, so I said to myself, Joe I said, it's okay because 'Arry'll pick 'im up the other side. You stick around. That's where I come to the funny turn up for the book, Mr Ar. You know what the lady did?"

Rollison felt as if he were choking.

"Tell me, Joe."

"She went right off to sleep."

"*What?*"

"Dead to the world," Joe assured him. "Now and again I got close enough to the window to take a dekko. She was okay, I could see 'er breaving, but sleep—talk about dead to the wide. They're just waking 'er up, Mr Ar— at least, they was when I come away to telephone."

"Joe, go and see her," said Rollison urgently. "Tell her to wait there until I come."

"Okay, Mr Ar."

"And that was a perfect report, Joe," Rollison remembered to praise, then slammed down the receiver and swung towards the door. He knew the hotel well, and also remembered seeing the restaurant in Moor Street, opposite the back entrance. Because parking would be difficult he did not take the car, but hurried towards Piccadilly; as he reached the corner he met an empty taxi. In ten minutes he was pulling up near the restaurant. He saw Joe outside, a short, stocky figure, wearing a badly-cut suit of light grey, rather shabby brown shoes, and a cloth cap; by him was a smart-looking new Vespa motor scooter, Joe's greatest pride. As Rollison got out, Joe's eyes lit up, and he gave the thumbs up sign; so at least Eve was all right.

He turned into the restaurant, with its green plants climbing up in the corners, a kind of imitation bamboo partition separating the dining-section from the counter service, the shiny red and black topped tables, the wicker-work chairs. He saw Eve sitting in a corner by herself, being watched from a distance by two waitresses; half a dozen people were sitting in the café, equally curious.

Eve looked up and saw him.

Dr Welling had been alarmed by her look of distress and near collapse; if he saw her now, he would order her straight to bed, and give her an injection to make sure

that she slept. Rollison went across to her. She looked
into his eyes, while her own eyes were covered with a film
of tears, and her lips trembled. He pushed two chairs out
of the way, sat down at the table, and took her hands,
holding them tightly. He realised then that above everything else he wanted desperately to see her.

"Rolly," she managed to say, "what have I done?"

16

BLAME?

THEY were back at Rollison's flat.

Joe Locket was in the kitchen, Welling was on the way, Rollison was sitting on the arm of the big chair in which Eve lay back. She was a little better than she had been, not so near breaking down, but her eyes were glassy and she could not keep still, even when Rollison was clasping her hand.

" . . . I could understand it more if we hadn't done exactly what he told us to," she said. "If you'd tried to follow him, or if you'd told the police—well, it would be understandable, wouldn't it? If we hadn't carried out our part of the bargain we couldn't be surprised that they didn't carry out theirs; but we did everything—at least *that's* not on my conscience. If we'd tried to follow them, or if you'd followed me, then I would just blame myself."

Rollison said: "You did everything you could."

"Yes," she said, and looked up at him, those glassy eyes still touched with beauty, her face pale and yet strangely calm. "So you were absolutely right: they couldn't be trusted. What do you think they'll do now?"

"They'll ask for more money," Rollison answered.

It was hard to get the words out, because of the simplicity of her trust, and because of what he knew; there was a chance that Max and Felix would have made the exchange—but for Joe and Harry. Joe and Harry might have been noticed, might have given the game away. So he might conceivably be to blame for this himself.

It was useless to keep insisting that it would have been crazy to trust the two brothers; as useless to tell himself that he could not possibly have allowed Eve to go away without making some attempt to help her. The truth was that she believed that they had carried out the terms implicitly; and they hadn't, because he hadn't thought it wise. Now he could almost hear himself talking to Ebbutt, just telling the man enough for the other two to work on. He should have gone himself. He should have been on tap to take a message the moment Eve arrived at the Astor Hotel. There was no one else to blame, no matter how he looked at the situation, and if he told her so, then—

He felt the nervous pressure of her fingers.

"What are we going to do now, Rolly?"

"I'm going to see Leah again," Rollison answered, "and you're going to rest."

"It's useless to expect me—" Eve began to protest.

"Eve, if you don't rest for a few hours you'll crack up completely."

"What about you?" she demanded. "You look as if you could fall asleep on your feet."

"I've been used to this kind of pressure for twenty years," Rollison told her, "so that's nothing to worry about. Dr Welling will be here very soon. You're going to do whatever he says."

"All right," Eve said, resignedly; and she obviously knew that she could not go on much longer. "Are you going to tell the police what happened?"

"Not yet. Not until I think it's vital."

"One thing's certain," Eve said; "you must do whatever you think best. Anything."

Rollison said: "I will, Eve." He sounded hoarse. When he stood up, he heard a sound of footsteps on the stairs; a moment later, he heard the ring at the front door bell, and felt sure that this was Welling, although there was a possibility that it was one of the men from the Yard; the Yard had been very quiet, except for sending that one man to see him earlier in the day.

It was Welling.

E

Welling had brought a hypodermic syringe and was going to stand no nonsense; Eve must sleep the clock round if she didn't want to collapse. Within five minutes he was dabbing at the tiny puncture in her arm with cotton wool soaked in spirit; within ten, she was getting into bed.

"But what she needs is freedom from her fear," Welling said. "I know you too well to ask questions, but if you want to save that woman from a complete nervous breakdown, then you've got to get rid of this fear. From what little I've seen of her, I would say she's been living on her nerves for a long time—years, possibly. Do you think you can help her?"

"I've got to help her," Rollison said simply.

Welling looked at him curiously, then said: "Well, don't knock yourself up in the process. This looks as if it's taking plenty out of you. I telephoned the hospital just before I came here," he went on, "and the report on Jolly couldn't be much better. I don't think you need worry about him at all. Any other way in which I can help?" he added, abruptly.

"Yes," said Rollison after a pause. "You can give me some sleeping tablets that will put me out cold in a few minutes."

"For you?" Welling demanded.

"Call it for me."

Welling gave him an old-fashioned look, and said: "Right. I'll send some over."

.   .   .   .   .

Eve was sleeping.

Percy Wrightson had arrived, a lanky, long-faced, lugubrious man, and had immediately telephoned to ask his wife to join him, to help 'look after the lady'. Joe Locket had gone home. There was no report from Harry Mills, and Rollison found himself thinking anxiously about the man, and remembering the ruthlessness with which the Hapley policeman, Jeff, had been run down. Rollison telephoned Ebbutt again; there was still no news. He put a call to Superintendent Grice of New Scotland Yard, but Grice was out on a bank hold-up job; his assistant told Rollison that there had been no trace of the driver of the Hillman, no trace of the driver of the Super Snipe. In short, the police had made no progress, and there was no particular reason why they should have done.

Rollison went out, left the Bentley outside the house, and took a Morris runabout from the mews garage; it would be much easier to handle in the rush-hour traffic. As he drove towards Kensington and the Marple Guest House, he found himself thinking not only of Eve, but of Caroline and her father. He had been consulted in the first place to look for Ralph Kane, and had given him hardly a thought.

Would it be easier to trace the girl through him?

Was he making a mistake in concentrating on Caroline through Leah—even if Leah were still at the guest house? He didn't think she would be; but there was always a chance that Max and his brother would be over-confident, feeling absolutely sure that he would not go to the police. He reached Marple Street and drove past the corner house, sure that he would not be recognised even if Max or Leah were there. He sat at the wheel, smoking. He was quite sure that he had not been followed, and he almost wished he had. There were so many anxieties crowding on him now; not least, Harry Mills. If anything had happened to Harry he would feel the full weight of blame.

He neared a corner, planning to park out of sight of the guest house, and saw an old Austin seven only fifty feet or so ahead, with a man sitting at the wheel. For the first time that day, Rollison's heart really leapt; for this was Harry Mills. He got out of the Morris and hurried over, while Harry looked straight ahead, as if completely

unaware that anyone was approaching him. Rollison
bent down and said:

"Haven't you got the price of a telephone call?"

"Cor lumme, it's Mr Ar!" exclaimed Harry, in a
squeaky voice. He was a small man, nearly fitting the
little old car, which was immaculate inside. His grey eyes
lit up, and he thrust his hand out of the window, to grip
Rollison's hand, "Want me to get out, or—"

"Stay there, and tell me what happened."

"Nothing much," answered Harry promptly. "That's
the worst of it. Once I got here, I was stuck. There isn't
any telephone kiosk in sight, and if I'd gone away to
find one, they might have skipped." He hadn't the same
pronounced Cockney accent as Joe, had a little round
bright face, and was very well dressed; Harry was also a
dandy. His black hair was brushed back in waves which
seemed to be Marcelled, and it glistened with a well-
advertised brand of pomade. "So I thought I'd better
stay put, Mr Ar."

"The man came here, did he?"

"He went half-way round London to get here, though."

"Did he stop on the way?"

"Nope," answered Harry. "Now and again he got held
up in traffic, but he's some driver, I can tell you that."

"Did he have a suitcase with him?"

"Brought it out of the Astor Hotel," answered Harry,
and told Rollison the same story that Joe had, up to the
point when Joe had gone round to the other side of the
hotel. "And he took it into the guest house, if that's the
right word for it." He sniffed.

"Isn't it, Harry?"

"Proper tarty lot have gone in and out there since I've
been waiting," Harry said scathingly. "Couple of old
dears, too, to be honest. Any instructions, Mr Ar?"

"Have you seen another man like the one you followed?"

"Nope."

"Have you seen a short, big-breasted girl—twenty-three or four, say—come out? Somewhere around 40, 22, 40."

Harry's eyes glistened.

"I wish I had!"

"Just stay here until I come back," said Rollison.

He left the car just round the corner from Harry's, and walked back to the Marple Guest House, keeping close to the small areas of the houses on that side of the street so that there was less chance of being seen from the window of Leah's room. It all seemed too good to be true: Max here, the money here, Leah here. Rollison reached the front door and found it wide open. There was a sound of frying and a smell of cooking, too. No one saw him. A breeze came in at the front door and made the theatre and cinema notices flap a little. He passed the first floor, and saw no one. As he approached the next floor, and room 7, he hesitated, watching all the other doors and looking behind him, in case he had been seen and was being watched.

There seemed to be no need for alarm.

He reached number 7. His heart thumped now, because there was the possibility of finding the money, as well as Max.

He turned the handle of the door, and thrust; and the door opened. Warning rose very high in his mind, for there was no longer any doubt: it was too easy, and that probably meant that it was being made easy. He thrust the door hard back against the wall, and it banged noisily, making pictures shake and oddments on the dressing-table rattle; but there was no sound.

The bed, made, was empty. The curtains were back and the blind was up. The room looked surprisingly bright and fresh, and had a well-kept appearance. There was a slight scent of roses. He looked into every corner, heart hammering because he was so sure that it was too easy.

Then he saw a suitcase.

It stood between the bed and the far wall. It looked new; and Joe had told him that the case which Eve had taken was a lightweight air-luggage case, a pale biscuit colour. Could it be full? He did not believe that anyone, even a pair as sure of themselves as Max and Felix, could be so careless; if it were full then the room was being watched and they knew that he was here. How could he be watched, except from the door? He glanced up at the ceiling and at the walls, seeing if there were a spy hole of any kind; it would be easy enough. He saw none. He went out and looked round, down the stairs and along the passages, and the place seemed deserted; there was that sizzling sound of frying and the appetising smell.

He reached the case.

There was room for someone to hide under the bed, of course, although no one could move easily and freely from there and he did not think it was likely; yet he turned up the drape of the bedspread carefully, feeling a little absurd; he saw only the cheap carpet. There was positively nowhere else that anyone could hide and from where they could surprise him, so he picked up the case.

It was as light as a case could be; empty.

He knew that the moment he touched it, yet he put it on the bed, turned the key and opened it, taking great care not to put his prints on the chromium plated locks. He eased the lid back. Yes, it was empty. Eve had told him that there had been four packets and it would be easy to take four separate packets out of the house; that was why Harry had noticed nothing. Rollison had a curiously flat feeling of disappointment, although all the time he had tried to persuade himself that he would not find the money.

Nor did he expect to find Leah.

But there was one other possibility: Max's room. There were only two men's names on the board downstairs, and one was against room number 12. A Mr M. Leon. 'M' for Max. Rollison went out, still feeling that he was being watched, yet unable to be sure. He went up the stairs. Now a radio had been switched on, and it sounded as if two men were talking. He reached the next floor; here were rooms 9 to 11; there was only one floor above. He hurried up the final flight, not really expecting to find Max; only he had to make every possible effort before he began to try to find Leah; and before he talked to Grice of the Yard.

The door of room 12 was closed and locked. Rollison hesitated, then took out his picklock, bent down and saw that the key was not inside the lock, so the tenant of this room was out. He had the door open in a few moments, and stepped inside a larger room than he had expected, and one which was comfortably furnished, where there was a 21" television set in a corner, a radio, rows of books, extremely comfortable arm-chairs; and there was a door leading to other rooms, the bedroom, bathroom and kitchen. He re-locked the door, then went into the bedroom, which was quite tiny, with just room for a bed, a small chair and a wardrobe. He opened the wardrobe and took out a suit; and he knew in a moment that this was not Max's room, nor Felix's; for the suit belonged to a much taller man.

Then he saw a photograph, standing on the window-sill, and even the Toff could hardly believe his eyes.

It was identical with the photograph on his desk; a print taken from the same negative. He stepped towards it and picked it up, just as he had picked up the one from his desk. Eve was smiling; Caroline, too: and only Ralph Kane had been straight faced when this photograph had been taken.

Who but Kane would have this photograph in his bedroom?

If Kane used this apartment when he was not at home, was his liaison with Leah more permanent than Eve realised?

If Kane lived here, did he know Max and Felix, and had he been a party to the kidnapping?

The thoughts were racing through Rollison's mind as he searched the apartment, finding nothing that helped him; no money, no papers, no letters, nothing except the photograph to point to the identity of the tenant. He had finished, and was trying to weigh the situation up when he heard a man approaching up the stairs.

17

RALPH KANE

ROLLISON stepped swiftly behind the door, waiting with increasing tension; there was a possibility that this man was going to pass the door, but it was not likely, and he did not think that the footsteps were those of either of the brothers. The man reached the landing, and came straight on. Outside there was a crash as if two cars had jolted together, and someone cried out, but Rollison had no time to think of that. He flattened himself against the wall, and dropped his right hand to his pocket.

A key was thrust into the lock.

The lock turned, and the door was pushed back slowly; it did not touch Rollison. A man stepped in, keeping his back to Rollison, and closed the door. A glance towards the right would be all that was needed; but he took the normal course when a door opened as this one did, and went further into the room.

He was taller than Rollison had expected, he had a lean figure, and he moved well. His hair was much greyer than Rollison had expected, too; silvery grey hair which waved a little, like the popular conception of an actor's. He thrust one hand into his pocket and jingled some coins, and went to the window. He stood looking out for a few seconds, the coins still jingling, upright, immaculate, the suit of pale grey that he was wearing looking as if it had been made by the world's best tailor. So far, Rollison had not been able to see his face, except for a glimpse of his profile; he had only the photograph to judge by, and he expected to see a very good-looking man.

Then, Kane turned round.

Rollison had moved forward a little, without a sound,

and was watching closely. He saw how right he was to have expected someone good-looking; this man was strikingly handsome.

Kane saw him, started violently, and raised his hands towards his chest, as if he expected an assault. He was older than Rollison had realised: in the early fifties. He stood with arms extended as if in boxing pose, mouth a little slack. The shock which had showed so clearly in his eyes faded; and the fact that Rollison made no move against him obviously took away his fear.

Rollison said: "Good evening, Mr Kane."

Kane said in a low-pitched voice: "Are you Richard Rollison?"

"Yes."

"I see." Kane pressed a hand against his forehead, and that gesture was remarkably like Eve's when she had been so tired, and when she had not known what to do. "I see," he repeated, and moved forward slowly. "They're always right. Always. Sometimes I think—"

He broke off.

"Who are always right?" asked Rollison.

"The Leonis," Kane answered. "Max and Felix Leoni." He pressed his hand against his forehead again, and went on: "They told me an hour ago that you would probably be in touch with me during the day. They always seem to know exactly what is going to happen—it's almost uncanny. I suppose it's what is called a sixth sense."

This man was tired, and worried; he was no middle-aged Lothario, buoyant and confident in his attractiveness to women, certainly no lady-killer—if he could be judged from his appearance now. He was a jaded, worried man, Rollison realised, and did not quite know why that surprised him so much.

"What else did they tell you?" asked Rollison.

Kane moved towards a cabinet on one wall, opened a cupboard, and showed an array of bottles and glasses. He took out whisky, a syphon of soda and two glasses.

His movements were smooth and easy; twenty years ago he must have been not only handsome but remarkably agile; the eligible batchelor of any girl's dream. Instead of answering, he said:

"What will you have?"

"Whisky will be fine," said Rollison.

Kane poured out, picked up soda, and said mechanically: "Say when." He brought Rollison the drink, then raised his glass to his lips; he didn't say a word more, but drank as if he were in urgent need of the stimulant. Rollison certainly was.

Then Kane said: "They told me that you would be here, and gave me a message for you."

It was easy to understand why he thought that the Leoni brothers had a sixth sense. It was easy to see, too, that he had taken the strong whisky and soda so as to brace himself; and now he looked straight into Rollison's eyes, his own shadowy; in that way, remarkably like Eve's. "They told me that unless you kept away from the police, and away from my wife, they would kill my daughter. And you've got to stay away, Rollison; you mustn't take any risk with Caroline's life."

Rollison said: "Well, well," and finished his drink. "So they're as frightened as that."

"*They're* frightened? What the devil do you mean?"

"If they weren't, they wouldn't throw that kind of threat about."

"You're wrong, Rollison," Kane said, very tensely. "You, and anyone else who underestimates the Leonis, is quite wrong. You've got to give up. You've got to leave me to work this out with my wife. It's essentially a family matter, and it won't help if you or the police become involved, in fact it will do terrible harm. They've part of what they want, now—twenty thousand pounds. They'll try to get more. But if the worst came to the worst they would kill Caroline, and get out of the country with the money they have already."

"You're more wrong than I am," Rollison said.

Kane moved towards the largest arm-chair, and sat on the arm of it, adjusted the line of his trousers, swung his leg a little, and then said:

"I don't care what reputation you have; I don't care how clever you think you are. You can't get the Leonis at the risk of my daughter's life. You've got to give up, Rollison. Where is my wife?"

"At my flat, under doctor's orders," Rollison answered, "and in good hands."

"Oh, I don't doubt that you mean well and will do the best you can," said Kane, still very tensely, "but you aren't equipped to handle men like the Leonis. You probably think that they have some decent qualities because they can be so smooth and pleasant. You couldn't be more wrong. They are murderous killers, they have absolutely no compunction, and if it would pay them to kill Caroline, or me or you, they would kill."

Rollison said quietly: "So we daren't let them get away with this."

"Yes, we can," barked Kane. "And we must. I've got to get my daughter back." He narrowed his eyes as he stood up, still speaking in a very level voice, and giving the impression that he meant every word. He poured himself another drink and tossed it down, then went on: "I don't know how much my wife has told you. I know she has been pretty strung up lately, living on her nerves, and it wouldn't surprise me if she had told you the truth —or her side of it. There might be one or two things that would surprise you, and even surprise her." He sounded very bitter. "I'd rather lose my own life than take any risks with Caroline's. Caroline is the one real thing salvaged out of the wreck of our marriage. Oh, she's Eve's child; I wouldn't make the slightest attempt to get her away, any more than I am prepared to take any risks with her life. I know these men too well." He shivered, as if he were looking upon horror. "Have you told the police about the money?"

"Not yet."

For the first time a glint appeared in Kane's eyes, as if he were both relieved and glad to hear that.

"And you're not going to," he declared, and put the empty glass down. "I know exactly what the Leonis want, and they're going to get it."

"What do they want?" asked Rollison.

"Fifty thousand pounds," Kane answered.

"Your wife's money?"

"Yes."

"You're very generous with it."

"If it were a hundred thousand it would make little or no difference to her."

"It's still her money."

"And it's our child."

"Why didn't you tell her about this when you found out what they wanted?"

"I don't have to explain my actions to you, although I might have to Eve," Kane said slowly, "but you may as well know how this developed. I got to know the Leonis through Leah Soloman, the girl you saw here. They discovered that my wife was a wealthy woman. They tried to blackmail me, over Leah. They came to realise that I really hadn't any money of my own. They suggested that I should get a large sum from my wife, saying that if I didn't get it for them, they would injure Caroline. I refused." He pressed his hand against his forehead again. "I not only refused, but said that I would go to the police. You see," he added, and there was an ugly twist to his lips, "I didn't know the Leonis then. I wish to God I had. It might have saved Caroline from this horror—" He broke off. "Never mind that. I've told you enough to show that I mean exactly what I say."

"How well do you know the Leonis now?" asked Rollison quietly.

"I've seen Caroline," Kane answered. "I've seen how ruthless they are. I know they ran down that policeman. I've seen—" He hesitated, and then stood up and clenched his fists and strode towards Rollison, eyes flashing, looking a younger, fiercer man, as if the recollection of what he had seen so horrified him that it gave him a new vigour to fight against it. "I know what they do to other girls. *I tell you, I know what they do!* I didn't realise it until recently, I didn't realise what I was helping them to do. They traffic in women. They ship young girls to North Africa and to South America, they—good God, Rollison, *you* don't need telling what goes on, or what happens to a girl who gets into the hands of devils like these."

Rollison said, slowly: "No, I don't need telling."

"Then have some sense, and get off this case."

"If the Leonis are as bad as you say they are, they've got to be caught."

"That's right," said Kane, his voice harsh with bitterness—"that's the kind of stiff-necked fool you are. You forget you're dealing with human beings, with creatures of flesh and blood—you're not just dealing with a principle. It doesn't matter a damn to me what happens to the Leonis or what they do to other people—all I want is to get Caroline back, and make sure that no harm can come to her. I can do it, and make sure that nothing else goes wrong. You haven't a chance."

Rollison just watched the man, seeing the glitter fade from his eyes, as if the recollection of fear soon conquered his anger. The Leonis could not have wanted a better spokesman—and in a way it was easy to understand him. If he felt for his daughter as keenly and as deeply as he said, then he would take any risks to save her; and the risk of losing another thirty thousand pounds of his wife's fortune was hardly one to worry him.

There was one good thing in this for Rollison: the Leonis had never intended to exchange Caroline for twenty thousand pounds; they might say they had; they might blame Rollison for having them followed, so as to exert more pressure on Eve; but it wasn't true. They had always been after this fifty thousand pounds—or more—had always felt quite sure that they would get it.

"So I haven't a chance," Rollison said, very slowly. "Kane, how wrong can you be? If they've got Caroline, if they're that kind of people, what guarantee have you got that for another thirty, another fifty or another hundred thousand pounds, they'll let her go?" He saw the glitter back in Kane's eyes as he went on: "There's just one way of getting Caroline back safely: that's finding her and fetching her away."

"All they want—"

"Don't be a credulous fool! They'll keep squeezing until your wife hasn't any money left. Look what they've done to her already, and look what they've done to you: you're both physical wrecks, you're both on the point of a mental and physical breakdown. You can't fight men like the Leonis, you're not equipped to try; and if they look like being too tough, I can get help from the police. Try to make up your mind—"

Kane said: "Rather than let you tell the police, Rollison, I will kill you. I'm quite sure that if the police know about them, they'll kill Caroline before they get away. They have several escape routes ready, they'll have no difficulty in getting out of the country. I tell you I *know* what devils these men are. And I tell you that I would rather kill you than let you talk to the police."

As he spoke, he took an automatic pistol from his pocket.

18

MOOD TO KILL

KANE looked as if he meant what he said.

He held the gun tightly in his right hand, and covered Rollison, who was too far away to hope to push it aside, and too close for there to be any chance of missing. The door, closed, was two yards away from him. He looked into Kane's glittering eyes, saw the tension at his lips, and told himself that he must be very careful indeed, or the man would shoot to kill.

"Put that gun away, and don't be a fool," he said.

"You're not going to the police, Rollison."

"We've got to find your daughter. Do you know where she is?"

"I know just one thing—you're not going to tell the police about the Leonis."

"Kane—"

"It's no use arguing with me," Kane said, and menace was raw in his voice; Rollison had the impression that he was thinking not only more rapidly but more coherently and lucidly. Kane had been suffering from shock, and at first he had hardly known how to handle the situation; but he believed that he knew now. "I've got to be sure that you can't bring harm to Caroline."

"If you shoot me," Rollison argued, as if dispassionately, "the police will be here within a few minutes. When you're held on a charge of attempted murder, you won't be able to help your daughter or your wife."

"I won't be held," Kane said. "It's no crime to shoot a man caught stealing from your flat."

The gun was shaking a little, because Kane was shaking with tension, but it did not shift its direction, and a bullet fired from it now would strike Rollison in the chest or in the stomach. The danger had built up so slowly that Rollison had not recognised it, but now he knew that it was imminent and acute. Probably Kane had been working up to this; probably he had tossed down those two whiskies so as to brace himself to kill, not just to talk.

"Don't do it, Kane," Rollison said, calmly enough. "Put the gun away, and let us work out the best way to help Caroline."

"I know the best way to help her."

"If you shoot me you won't be able to help Caroline, yourself or Eve."

Then, Rollison knew that he had made a mistake.

The name 'Eve' had come out unbidden, and it seemed to stab at Kane. He saw the glitter back in the man's eyes. He saw the way his lips twisted. He saw the gun thrust forward, the forefinger on the trigger. He was quite sure that Kane meant to shoot; that he was simply screwing himself up to do it, and the way Rollison had said 'Eve' gave him his final impetus. In a flash of intuition, Rollison realised something which he had not even suspected, which he did not believe Eve even suspected. *This man was still in love with his wife*, and all his *affaires* did not alter that.

The reason did not really matter, either. There was a possibility that he was anxious to turn his back on his old life and start afresh with his wife and daughter, but that was unimportant. He was in love with Eve, and now he hated Rollison—and there was almost certainly a deeper motive for his hatred than Rollison had realised until that moment.

Rollison's mouth was very dry.

"Kane," he said, "I can prove that I came here to see you—I've a man outside."

"You think you have," Kane sneered. "You think you're so brilliant, but you haven't a chance with the

Leonis. Your man's gone. Max Leoni knew that he was being followed all the time, let the man stay outside until you came here so that you would think that you would have help handy, and now he's dealt with him. That's something you can't get into your head, Rollison— there's no way of beating the Leonis. They know— everything." There was sweat on Kane's forehead now, and beads of sweat on his upper lip, and he did not appear to notice how Rollison was inching forward to make a desperate leap to thrust the gun away; a leap right or left would not save him. "He told me that Eve stayed the night at your flat, he told me that you behaved more like lovers than like friends, he told me that the quicker you were wiped off the face of the earth the better it would be for me, and by God he was right."

Rollison said: "Kane, he's lied to you all along, and if you believe him now—"

"I can believe the evidence of my own eyes and ears," Kane said. "*Stay where you are.*" He was ashen pale and, although his hand was still trembling, the forward thrust told Rollison that he was on the point of shooting; only a miracle could stop him now, and Rollison did not believe in that kind of miracle. "I've got one chance of making something of my life, and you're not going to rob me of it."

Rollison said, suddenly, almost brokenly: "All right, Kane, have it your own way."

He saw the glint of surprise in the other's eyes, and won the only chance he would get: a moment's respite, while Kane's tension was relaxed, and when his finger was not touching the trigger.

Rollison jumped forward.

Alarm came in place of surprise, the automatic wavered and described a circle, and for an awful moment it was pointing straight at Rollison's eyes; if Kane fired now he could not miss. Then, Rollison reached him and pushed the gun aside; at the same moment it went off, and the bullet buried itself in the floor. The report sounded deafening, and Kane tried to swing the gun round to shoot again.

Rollison struck him with a clenched fist to the stomach, using all the force at his command. He heard him gasp with pain as he staggered back. Rollison grabbed at his right wrist, gripped it, and twisted; the gun dropped to the carpet with a thud, and lay close to Rollison's foot. He did not kick it, but went after Kane, hitting him twice more, making sure that he could not put up a fight. Then he stopped the man from falling, and lowered him into the big arm-chair; doing so, he knocked a glass off the arm; it fell but did not break.

Rollison drew back, bent down and picked up the automatic, then put his knuckles to his lips. He was sweating, and felt a sickening reaction; he would never be nearer death, and survive. But there were other things to worry about; Harry Mills for one, and the effect of the sound of the shot on people who lived in the house. Some were bound to have heard it, and there was a risk that someone would send for the police and come to find out about it afterwards. He went to the door, listened, and heard a woman call out shrilly:

"Did you hear that?"

"It sounded like a gun going off," another woman called back.

"That's what it was. Where did it come from?"

"Upstairs," a woman declared.

"I *thought* it was out in the street," put in another.

"No, I'm sure it was in the house somewhere."

Rollison opened the door, stepped out and called down in a voice which he hoped was a passable imitation of Kane's.

"Hope I didn't scare anyone. I was cleaning a lamp, and dropped the bulb. No harm done. Damned silly of me. Sorry." Before anyone could peer up and see him, he backed away. He closed the door with a bang, hoping against hope that the explanation would satisfy them, and afterwards he heard only a mutter of voices. He crossed to the window. Kane was lying back in the chair, still looking dazed; he was likely to stay like that for several minutes. Rollison opened the window and leaned out as far as he could, looking towards the corner, and the spot where he had left Harry.

He saw a crowd of people, but the Austin was out of sight.

He felt his heart thumping again, and found himself recalling what Kane had said about the omniscience of the Leonis. He had come up against men like these before; men who considered every move they made so carefully and yet were able to adapt themselves to changed circumstances so quickly, that they seemed abnormally efficient, and were therefore doubly dangerous.

He turned back to Kane, poured out a weak whisky and soda, and held it in front of the man's face. Kane eased himself up to a more comfortable sitting position, and sipped. The dazed look in his eyes was gone, and there was hatred in the way he stared at Rollison.

Rollison asked sharply: "What did they do with the man in the Austin?"

"I don't know," muttered Kane.

"Get this clear, Kane," Rollison said. "If the Leonis hurt him, not all the danger to your daughter or your wife will stop me from going to the police. Do you know where to get in touch with the Leonis?"

"Yes," Kane muttered.

"Where?"

"I've a telephone number."

"When I've gone, telephone them and tell them I want Harry Mills and his Austin released and outside my flat by seven o'clock tonight, or I'll be talking to Scotland Yard by one minute past seven. Is that clear?"

"Yes," Kane said, and went on as if bitterly: "You don't really give a damn about my wife or daughter, do you?"

Rollison answered, as if the taunt didn't affect him: "I've known Mills for a long time. Do you know where Caroline is?"

Kane didn't answer.

"Do you know?"

"Yes," he muttered. "Yes, but—"

"You've succeeded in doing one thing," said Rollison harshly. "You've persuaded me that I ought to try and get her myself, and not call on the police unless it becomes desperate."

"There's no need for you to do anything! I can get Caroline back—"

"I don't believe it," Rollison said. "I don't believe they will hand her over for any sum of money. I believe they've got you exactly where they want you, and they'll bleed you and your wife dry. Where is Caroline?"

Kane didn't answer.

Rollison moved towards the telephone, saw the alarm in Kane's eyes, saw him start to get out of his chair, and then drop back into it again. Rollison picked up the receiver, looking at Kane all the time, and dialled; and as he dialled he uttered the letters and the numerals.

"W-H-I-1-2-1-2."

All the world knew that was Scotland Yard; and Kane, watching his fingers, knew that it wasn't bluff, and that he had actually dialled the Yard. Rollison waited, with the receiver an inch or two from his ear; suddenly the operator at the Yard answered, and the sound filtered out into the room.

Kane jumped up from his chair and tried to leap at Rollison, but he was still winded and hurt, and he staggered and nearly fell.

"Scotland Yard," repeated the operator aloofly.

"Superintendent Grice, please," Rollison said. "This is Roll—"

"Don't do it!" cried Kane, and this time he managed to reach Rollison and to clutch at his right hand and the telephone; but Rollison held him off. "For God's sake don't do it! I'll tell you where she is. I'll tell you, but don't let the police—"

"I'm sorry, but Mr Grice isn't in his office. He's still out on a case," the girl said. "I can give you Mr Appleton."

Rollison said: "I'll call later."

He rang off, and saw the perspiration pouring down Kane's forehead. Kane was breathing very hard, too; There was no doubt that he had reached a peak of terror. He was in such a condition that it would be impossible to rely on him; once Rollison had gone, he would tell the Leonis that he had promised to take Rollison to Caroline—

Did he know where the girl was?

Was he right about the evil that was in the Leonis?

They had certainly convinced him of the horrors which were in store for Caroline if he refused to obey them.

Kane muttered: "Rollison, I don't care what you do, but don't tell the police. It will be absolutely fatal."

"Where is she?" demanded Rollison.

"I–I can take you there, but—"

"*Where is she!*"

"For God's sake don't make me tell you," Kane begged. "Why don't you believe me when I say that there isn't a chance for her unless we pay that extra money? What does it matter to you if my wife pays? I tell you it won't make any difference to her—she has nearly a quarter of a million! There have been times when I wished to God she hadn't, but she has it—and she wouldn't care how much she paid for Caroline. Why don't you leave us alone and let us settle this our own way?"

Rollison asked expressionlessly: "Where is Caroline?"

"I'm not going to tell you? I'll take you there, but if the Leonis knew I'd told you—"

"Kane," said Rollison, "you're going to tell me where to find Caroline, or I'm going to the police with the whole story."

Kane pressed the heels of his thumbs against his forehead as if the pain at his head and eyes was unbearable, and then he muttered:

"You don't know what you're doing. If they kill her, her life will be on your conscience for ever, and if—" He broke off, moistened his lips, and then went on: "She's at a cottage on the outskirts of Hapley. It's only three miles from the school. They rented it weeks ago. It's called the Thatch, a little thatched cottage on the Worcester Road, between Worcester and Hapley, just past an inn called the Double Horse, going from Hapley to Worcester. You can't miss it, even at night; there's an all-night service station by the inn. But if you try to go there, you'll be—"

He couldn't finish.

Rollison said: "All right, Kane, take it easy. What you need is eight hours' sound sleep, like your wife—and that's what you're going to get. Come on."

"I can't leave here! They're going to telephone me later. I've got to be in."

"They can telephone me," Rollison said firmly. "Come on." He took Kane by the arm just above the elbow and made him get up, and then hustled him across the room to the door. He unlocked the door and pulled it open and thrust Kane forward—and Kane almost fell against Leah, who backed hastily away.

And behind Leah was Max Leoni.

Max said brightly: "You two weren't thinking of going anywhere, were you?" He stood at the top of the stairs, so that it would be impossible to get past without pushing him to one side. "Turn back into the flat, Kane," he ordered. "Don't let Rollison fool you. The price is too high. Isn't it, Leah?"

19

CHOICE

It seemed to Rollison that he had never seen such pleading on the face of a woman; nor such agony of mind showing in the face of a man. Only Max was happy, with the broad smile which made his white teeth gleam and which seemed to suggest that he was absolutely sure of himself.

Leah stepped towards Rollison with one hand outstretched; and for the first time he noticed what small, white hands she had. She looked older, in her pleading, and he felt quite sure that she believed what she said. Her pouty little mouth was trembling, the only colour in her face was at her lips and her eyes, shaded with pale blue.

"Don't let him hurt Caroline," she pleaded. "Don't get in his way, Mr Rollison. You've no idea what he will do if you try."

"Or possibly he has a faint idea, being a man of the world," smiled Max.

"For God's sake, Rollison, give it up," Kane begged. "If you had a daughter of your own, you'd know what I feel like now. If I had a million pounds I'd spend it to save Caroline!"

"That's the kind of talk I like to hear," said Max. "He means it, Rollison—just as I mean it when I tell you that the girl will be on your conscience for the rest of your life if you don't do what Kane advises."

Leah almost sobbed: "I beg you not to fight him any more."

And Max beamed—

Rollison could not understand the man's bounding confidence and assurance; it was as if he knew that he could do nothing wrong; was certain to win. From the beginning he had been absolutely sure that this was going according to plan: the Leonis' plan.

Rollison still had a hold on Kane, who stood a little to one side. Both men and the girl were staring at him, as if determined by their combined will-power to make him give way; for a few seconds, faced with a choice which he hated, he felt almost as desperate as Kane and Leah. Then, gradually, a new mood came. The Leoni brothers had pushed Kane into a corner; pushed Eve there, too; and Leah. They had used a kind of psychological pressure which had terrorised them all, and now Max was trying the same tactics on him.

He had come very close to success.

There was Jolly, there were Rollison's feelings towards Eve, and there was his own fatigue. There was his anxiety about Harry Mills, too, and the dark and frightening background to it all, the fear of what might happen to Caroline.

It was Max's smile which brought about the change of mood and the change of tactics.

Rollison gave a quick, flashing grin; it did not match Max's, but it startled him, and obviously Leah could not believe what she saw, for she backed away, as if in alarm. Kane exclaimed, but did not move. Rollison's smile broadened because of the puzzlement in Max's eyes, as he said:

"Very sure of yourself, Max, aren't you?"

"I'm sure," Max said.

Rollison let Kane go, and Caroline's father took a step to one side. Max did not seem satisfied, and he was frowning, the groove between his thick black eyebrows, cutting very deep.

"Have it your own way," Rollison said lightly. He seemed as sure of himself as Max, and for the moment he even felt relief from fear. "You can have Kane, you can have Leah, you can keep the twenty thousand pounds and you can even have Caroline—if you'll take the risk. That's up to you."

Max was staring at him, dull-eyed now; trying to see the reason for this change.

"What risk?" demanded Kane, harshly.

"The obvious risk," Rollison said brightly. "Either you come with me, or I go to the police. If I go to the police, you may harm Caroline, but you'll throw away your only chance of collecting the money you want—and on my evidence alone, the police would charge you." Rollison took Kane's gun out of his pocket, held it lightly in his right hand, and moved towards the head of the stairs. He had no idea at all how this would work out, but Max might realise how deadly it would be if the police were brought in. The man's smile had turned into a frown, and he did not move, but still blocked the head of the stairs. Rollison kept the gun lightly in his right hand, and went straight towards Max, who looked as if he would stand there and force the issue.

At the last moment, Max stood aside.

"Thanks," Rollison said, without looking round. "Come on, Kane." He accepted the danger that Max carried a gun and would shoot; but if he showed fear or any sign of weakness, he knew that he would undo any good that the last few seconds had done. He had seized the initiative, and if Max allowed him to keep it, then it was almost certain that Max was nothing like so sure of himself as he made out.

Rollinson went down a flight of stairs and stopped on the landing; now he could turn round without giving any impression that he was frightened. He saw the three of them standing high above his head; Kane and the woman aghast, Max empty handed. Rollison slipped the gun into his pocket, and said:

"It's now or never."

Kane exclaimed: "Leoni, you've got to stop him from going to the police!"

Rollison didn't speak but looked away; a long stretch of drab brown lino-covered stairs was ahead of him, and he started down slowly, wanting to plead with Kane to come but knowing that the first sign of weakness would be dangerous. He was half-way down the stairs when Kane burst out:

"*Stop him!*"

Max Leoni said: "You go with him, Kane, but don't talk; understand that? Don't talk."

Kane gasped: "You mean—"

"You heard what I said."

Rollison felt nearer exulting than he had for a long time, but he did not show it and he did not turn round again until he reached the foot of the next flight of stairs. Then he saw Kane coming slowly down, heard his footsteps, and heard Leah say something without being answered.

"What happened to my man in the Austin?" Rollison demanded.

Now, Max sneered: "He met with a slight accident, and he's on the way to hospital, but don't get excited—he wasn't hurt badly."

"What hospital?"

"Central London."

Rollison said: "I'll come back and see you if he's hurt badly," and started down the next flight of stairs, with Kane at his heels; a thoroughly bewildered Kane. Rollison stepped into the street and there was tension and anxiety in his mind as he looked towards the corner. The Austin had been struck by a battered Hillman, both the cars were locked together at the bumpers, and a crowd had gathered round; but there was no sign of an ambulance. Rollison remembered the crash he had heard, and knew that this had happened just after he had gone into Kane's room; it had been perfect timing at a point when Max had seemed completely sure of himself.

What was he doing now?

Telephoning his brother?

Rollison crossed to the other side of the road. A little woman with fluffy grey hair was saying in a shrill voice:

"And I saw it with my own eyes; it's a wonder that poor man wasn't killed outright. Sitting there reading the newspaper he was, and that *fool* ran into him. He *said* he was trying to avoid a dog, but I didn't see a dog anywhere near at the time, and I saw everything with my own eyes."

"You ought to make a statement to the police," a younger woman said.

The time might come when Rollison would want to talk to this grey-haired woman, but this wasn't it. He guided Kane round the corner to the Morris, which no one appeared to have touched. He said: "Wait a minute," and opened the driving door with great caution, making sure that there were no booby traps, then went to the front of the car and put up the bonnet; nothing appeared damaged. "All right," he went on to Kane, and the two tall men sat side by side in the little car, heads almost touching the roof, knees jammed beneath the dashboard.

"Why did you do that?" asked Kane.

"There's always a possibility that Max would put a firework in the engine, to scare the wits out of me," Rollison replied, and added mildly: "Or to blow me to smithereens. I don't like Max any more than you do."

Kane said, slowly and reluctantly: "I have to admit that I didn't dream he would let me come with you. You judged him better than I did."

"Max is worried," Rollison remarked, yet wondered if he were fooling himself. He was thinking fast as he went on, almost mechanically, not only talking to Kane, but trying to convince himself. "I think that his brother will soon be worried, too. They want more money and they're beginning to think they might not get it. When anyone makes such a point of trying to keep you away from the police, there's only one obvious reason: they're really frightened of the police. In short—"

He was almost glad when Kane interrupted.

"Do you mean they actually have police records? They're vulnerable?"

"Would it surprise you?" asked Rollison dryly. "The thing that matters is that they've got Caroline."

"Yes," said Kane, and pressed his hand against his forehead again, in that gesture which was so reminiscent of Eve. "If they're so vulnerable, why have they come out into the open as they have? Max gave me the impression that he wasn't frightened of anything or anybody."

"That's what he set out to do." Rollison turned into Kensington High Street, and appeared to be preoccupied with traffic, so he didn't go on; but he was asking himself over and over again: 'Why is Max so sure? And why did he give in so easily?'

Then a new thought flashed: anyone could see how near breaking point Kane was. Max must have realised that he would probably talk—and would talk about the cottage. It was almost as if Max and his brother, thinking several moves ahead, intended Rollison to know where Caroline was.

Could that be true?

The traffic thinned out near Kensington Gardens, and most of the cars were coming in the opposite direction.

"This doesn't make any difference to Caroline's danger," Kane was saying. "They're bound to guess that I'll tell you where she is, so they're almost certain to get her away from that cottage."

"It could be," conceded Rollison.

"Then the situation will be worse, not better."

"They have a big problem, Kane," said Rollison, still trying to convince himself. "They have to turn twenty thousand pounds in notes into easily portable quantities. They're not sure whether I've been to the police or not, and they're wondering whether all the ports and airfields will be watched. They don't know which way to jump, and they don't know which way I'll jump if they do Caroline any harm."

After a pause, Kane agreed: "I suppose not. Are you going straight down to the cottage?"

"Yes."

"I'm coming with you," Kane said.

Rollison glanced round, saw the set line of his jaw, and the feverish brightness of his eyes. This was the man who, not long ago, had tried to shoot him. This was a man who was beside himself, and he could not be relied on to take any rational course. This was the man who had been utterly faithless to a wife whom he loved. Rollison turned into Gresham Terrace, pulled up, and saw one of Bill Ebbutt's lightweights, a perky sparrow of a man, leaning against a lamp-post and reading an evening newspaper; he grinned and waved to Rollison as he strolled across.

"Bill sent me along to make sure nuffink goes wrong," he said, and looked curiously at Kane. "You okay, Mr Ar?"

"Fine, thanks," Rollison said. "Nip along to the nearest telephone, Micky, tell Bill that Harry Mills was mixed up in a car smash, and that he's at the Central London Hospital, but not badly hurt." The little boxer's eyes narrowed, and he looked alarmed. "Get back as soon as you can."

"Oke," Micky said, and went hurrying.

"Who was that?" asked Kane, staring after him.

"You'll find out I've got a lot more friends than Max and Felix have," said Rollison. "Come on." He hurried up the stairs and, as he reached the top landing, the door opened and Percy Wrightson appeared, smiling what was intended to be a polite smile of welcome but was really a widespread grin; he had always enjoyed acting *locum* for Jolly. "Hallo, Percy," greeted Rollison. "Get me the Central London Hospital on the telephone, will you?"

"Yep."

"Any messages?"

"No, sir," said Percy, suddenly remembering his position, and he inclined his head slightly as Rollison ushered Kane in. He saw Kane glance round the large room, his gaze resting for a moment on the Trophy Wall; and then Kane demanded:

"Where is my wife?"

"This way," Rollison said, and took him across the room and to the spare bedroom, opened the door, saw that the blinds were drawn—and a moment later saw a little bundle of a woman, Mrs Wrightson, peering at him from the kitchen doorway.

"She hasn't stirred, so I look in every half-hour to make sure she's all right," she whispered.

"Thanks," said Rollison, and watched Kane's face as he stepped inside and saw Eve.

20

SPEED

KANE approached the bed slowly, almost falteringly. Rollison had no doubt at all of the depth of his feeling, then; he looked a broken man. He stood by the side of his wife, hands held out towards her, as if he longed to take her in his arms, and he seemed oblivious of Rollison as he bent down, touched Eve's shoulders lightly, and pressed his lips against her forehead. But she did not stir. Her face was turned towards Rollison and the door, and she looked as lovely as he had ever seen her; and resting, too.

Wrightson called: "I got the 'orspital, Mr Ar."

Rollison hesitated, then turned away and closed the door. Wrightson was standing in the doorway, obviously on edge because the hospital was waiting.

"Thanks," Rollison said heavily. "Pour out two double whiskies, and have one yourself."

"With Aggie around? Not on your life," rejoined Wrightson. "I wouldn't mind a beer, though."

"Help yourself."

"Ta," said Wrightson, and drew himself up as Rollison lifted the receiver. "Thank you very much, sir."

Rollison asked first for the casualty ward, and as he held on he was picturing Eve's face, in the pose he had seldom seen, and the tension in Kane. The casualty ward answered.

". . . Mills, sir, yes, came in about an hour ago. Oh, not very serious, he'll be going home in the morning, if not tonight."

"That's fine," Rollison said, with real relief. "Now give me the private ward sister's office, will you?" Although he told himself that there would have been word from Welling if Jolly had taken a turn for the worse, he was on edge until he was assured.

"Comfortable and quite as well as would be expected, Mr Rollison."

"Thanks," Rollison said, and this time his relief was fervent. "You've been very good." He rang off, went straight to his desk, took out the tablets which Welling had given him and, in front of Wrightson's popping eyes, put two into one of the whiskies, and crushed them with the end of a fountain pen. "Soda, Percy," Rollison said, and winked, and with a husky voice Wrightson said: "You certainly are a one, Mr Ar! I must say the chap looks as if he could do with some shut-eye." He put the syphon of soda near the two glasses, and Rollison went back to the bedroom. Kane had moved to the window, and was staring at the houses opposite, his head held high, his hands clenched by his side. He heard Rollison, turned, and said stiffly:

"I owe you an apology, Rollison. No one could have looked after my wife more thoroughly. Thank you."

"Now come and have a drink," Rollison said.

. . . .

Ten minutes later, Kane was as deeply asleep as his wife.

"Percy," Rollison said.

"Yes, sir?"

"When I've gone out, I want you to lock the door and open it only to people you know. Don't let anyone else in. You know Dr Welling, don't you?"

"The old doc? Sure, I know *him*."

"And you know the trick mirror?"

Percy Wrightson winked . . .

The trick mirror was set in the wall above the front door, and by glancing up it was possible to see who was outside. That was one of Jolly's ideas, and had been installed for some time. Rollison was quite sure that

F

Wrightson would not take the slightest unnecessary risk, and it was safe to go out.

He went to his desk, and telephoned the Yard; and although it was late, Superintendent Grice was at his desk.

". . . yes, I'm handling the case," Grice said. "We still haven't found that Hillman, but—"

"Forget it for now, will you?" Rollison pleaded. "Bill, will you play ball if I give you some off-the-record information?"

"You could try me."

"I daren't risk it going too far," Rollison said. "The girl might be killed if her kidnappers know that you're on to them."

Grice said in a quiet voice: "What do you want us to do, Rolly?"

"Watch all ports and airfields for the Kane girl," Rollison answered, "and go through the Rogue's Gallery and take out all the black-haired men, standing about five feet five to seven, southern European type, current names Max and Felix Leoni, and let me have the photographs—"

Grice exclaimed: "*Leoni?*", as if he were aghast.

"Know them?" Rollison barked.

"Are you sure they're involved?"

"Positive."

"Rolly," Grice said, gruffly, "be very careful how you handle the Leonis. The police of several countries have been trying to get a charge against them for a long time, but haven't succeeded. They operate between here and Central and Southern Europe, and between France, North Africa and South America. They are known to kidnap young girls and hold them to ransom, but we've never found proof. They have another favourite trick, of arranging engagements for dancers and singers on attractive terms, and outwardly they're genuine. But—" Grice hesitated, and then went on with a vehemence which seemed greater because he spoke so quietly: "They are vicious and deadly, and we want proof against them badly." He paused again. "I can tell you that you're right about one thing: if they make a threat, they carry it out."

"They don't know that I'm talking to you," Rollison reminded him. "Bill—"

"Yes?"

"There was a little street accident in Marple Street this afternoon or early this evening. One of Bill Ebbutt's men was slightly hurt. His car was hit by a Hillman." He heard Grice draw in a sharp breath, and went on: "The driver of the Hillman said that he swerved to avoid a dog, but there's at least one woman in the street who didn't see the dog although she saw the accident. If you could get on to that driver, you might find that he ran down Jeff, at Hapley. If he did, you can get at the Leonis this way, and not through me. Will you try?"

"I'm ringing *Accidents* on the other line," Grice said. "Rolly, be very careful."

"I'll be careful," Rollison assured him.

He rang off, hesitated, became aware of Percy Wright-son staring at him, and saw Percy's wife coming in with a large plate of luscious looking ham sandwiches. He was taking one when the telephone bell rang.

"Put those in a box for me, I'll eat them as I'm driving," he said, and hesitated again, then lifted the telephone. "Rollison speaking." He expected to hear one of the Leonis, but was not really surprised when a woman spoke to him; he felt quite sure that it was Leah.

"I've got a message for you," she said. She was breathing hard, and gave the impression that someone whom she feared was standing close by her side. "From—from Max. Can you hear me?"

"Yes."

"He says he'll make the exchange for another twenty," Leah said. "He says that you've made it too hot for them, and they'll do a deal this time."

"Leah," said Rollison, and she answered in a gasping voice:

"Yes?"

"Tell them I'm going to the cottage. Tell them that I'm going to bring Caroline away with me. Tell them that I've posted a letter to my bank, explaining everything and naming them, and it will be opened unless I talk to the bank by nine o'clock in the morning. Have you got all that?"

"I—no, not all of it!" She almost screamed. "Tell me it again, more slowly." He told her, and she repeated it word for word. Then: "They've gone out, but they'll want to know all about this the moment they're back," she went on. "They'll—they'll want you to bring the other twenty with you. Mr Rollison, don't make any mistake about it, *please*. He means what he threatens to do to Caroline Kane if you don't bring that money."

"I can believe it," Rollison said.

"They—they're devils!" Leah burst out. "They—"

She rang off, as if afraid that she was saying too much.

Rollison saw Mrs Wrightson come in, with a cardboard box containing the sandwiches, and a thermos flask which she was screwing up as she approached. Rollison said: "Thanks, Aggie. Keep an eye on Percy and make sure he does his job properly," and went out, to Aggie's delighted smile and Percy's pretended disgust. He glanced up at the mirror; no one was outside. He went slowly down the stairs. The Rolls-Bentley was standing outside, near the Morris. All the time he was thinking of the way Leah talked of the Leonis; of the effect they had on Grice; of the effect they had on Ralph Kane. It was true that when he had called Max's bluff, he had won a minor victory, but Caroline was still in the Leonis' hands, and no one who knew anything about them doubted the gravity of her danger.

Rollison saw a small car, an open M.G., parked further along the street, and at once he remembered Joe Locket

telling him about the M.G. which had been near the
Astor Hotel. He walked towards it, and was twenty yards
away when he recognised Max. He did not hesitate, but
went straight up to him.

Max was back to normal, smile flashing.

"You get my message about a little matter of another
twenty thou?"

"I got it."

"You've also got quite a problem," Max said. "How
would you get hold of twenty thousand pounds at this
time of day?"

"If I really wanted it I would go to Harting's, the
jewellers, in New Bond Street," Rollison answered
promptly. "He lives above his shop. If he hadn't the cash
he would let me have diamonds up to that amount."

"I would lose on the exchange," Max objected quickly.
"Make it thirty thousand pounds' worth of diamonds.
Don't get me wrong, Rollison. It's the money for the
Kane girl. If you don't play it our way, she'll have her
throat cut tonight."

He actually smiled again, as if at a great joke.

Rollison said harshly: "What diamonds or money I can
get, I'll take to the cottage. You can have them in
exchange for Caroline."

"And little Eve will pay you back tomorrow, will she?"

"I'll get paid back," Rollison said. He turned away,
got into the Rolls-Bentley and, as he turned the corner,
saw the M.G. move after him. It was just behind him when
he reached the jewellers, but he ignored it while he waited
for old Harting to answer his call. A voice came from a
hidden loudspeaker fitted in the door.

"Who is that, please?"

"Hallo, Harty," Rollison said, into a hidden micro-
phone. "Remember me?"

"It is Mr Rollison!" the speaker exclaimed. "I will
release the door at once. Come up, do come up."

The door opened, and Rollison stepped inside a dark,

narrow hall. The door closed behind him, electrically controlled, and a light went on at the top of a flight of narrow stairs. An elderly, white-haired man beckoned him.

After a warm greeting, Harting asked:

"And what is it you need, my friend?"

Rollison said easily: "Twenty thousand pounds' worth of small diamonds, Harty, and an insurance cover for them; and twenty thousand pounds' worth of imitation . . ."

The old man's eyes lit up.

The M.G. was still outside when Rollison went downstairs, with two washleather bags in his pocket, one sealed, the other tied at the neck. The car followed him across the heart of London as far as the Edgware Road, and then it disappeared from his driving mirror.

He put his foot down as hard as he dare.

He found himself thinking of the first trip to Hapley—only last night. It seemed a year ago. Eve, sitting next to him, trying to relax. The whole case stretched out in front of him; and it had looked like a domestic problem, a simple conflict of emotions!

It wasn't yet dark and he made better time than he had the previous night, but it was pitch dark when he reached Hapley and drove through the little town towards Worcester. No car followed him and he did not believe that Max or any car on the road could have travelled faster than he had; but Felix and perhaps others would be at this cottage—unless he had allowed himself to be fooled. His headlights shone on telegraph wires, and turned the hedges and the trees to silver, until the neon lights and the illuminated pumps of a filling station appeared. Just beyond this was the Double Horse Inn, and soon the headlamp beams fell upon the thatch of a cottage which lay a little way back from the road. The window panes shone bright yellow for a moment, and then were lost in darkness. The headlights now shone on the top of a hedge and on a flower garden, all the blooms of which appeared to be robbed of colour. There was ample room to park outside, and Rollison stopped. This was a moment when there were no other cars on the road, and there was no sound. He stepped out of his car. He could use the few pounds' worth of paste jewels with him, or the genuine stones, and he did not know whether the paste would fool Felix, who might be knowledgeable about diamonds. He doubted whether he had been in greater danger. The Leonis believed that he had kept away from the police, so that if they killed him, there would be no danger to them. The obvious thing to believe was that they planned to kill him, take the diamonds, and also kill Caroline before they left, for she could identify one of them, or perhaps both, as well as Leah.

Rollison opened a small gate; and it creaked.

He found himself asking why he was taking this dreadful risk, and knew the answer before the question floated on the night air. It was not simply for the girl whom he had never met; and it was not simply because it was part of the job. No man alive could be expected to take such a risk for those reasons.

He was doing this for Eve.

He was doing this because she mattered to him; and she had from the moment he had seen her. He did not try to explain or to justify it. He saw her as she had kissed him, and could feel the pressure of her lips on his; and he saw her as she lay in bed, with Kane bending over her and kissing her, gently.

She would wake up to find hope dead; or hope renewed with almost wild exultation.

He walked up the little path, just able to make out the shape of the brass knocker, the letter-box and the bell; and he rang the bell, hearing the sound ring inside the cottage.

Then he waited.

21

FAIR EXCHANGE?

No light came on, and there was no sound, until a car came swishing past and Rollison was shown up in the headlights for a moment; after that the darkness seemed greater than before. He put a hand to the door and pushed; it did not yield. He found the handle, twisted and pushed; still the door did not open. He moved to one side, taking out the thin pencil torch he had used when he had come to Hapley last night. Little more than twenty-four hours ago the girl had been sitting happily in her study, with no idea of what was going to happen to her.

How great *was* his own risk?

Would the Leonis believe him about the letter to the bank? They were bound to know most of the tricks he was likely to use, and that one wasn't exactly novel. Its strength was that Leoni could not be sure either way.

His chief hope was that they would believe that they could get what they wanted and be safely away from here before nine o'clock in the morning, and be out of danger, but that if he died the police would be after them.

He put the thought of death behind him.

He saw the grass, the flower beds, still strangely colourless, and then a crazy-paving path which led to the back of the cottage. He walked round. There was a yellow light at a small window, and he went close and peered inside, but all he could see was an oil lamp shining on a polished table. He went on, and found the back door inside a little porch. He disturbed a bird or a bat, and it rustled, startling him. He stepped inside the porch, and there seemed to be no light at all when he switched off his torch. He tried the handle, turned and pushed—and the door opened.

Nothing else happened.

He shone the torch about a kitchen which had flag-stones on the floor, a huge dresser which seemed to take up the whole of one wall, and a small table. He banged against the table, and it scraped on the stone. He looked for an electric light switch, found one, pressed it down, and blinked in the bright light.

A door leading to the front part of the cottage was open. He stepped through it. Two doors led off a passage, one of them was ajar, and a pale yellow light shone through; this was the room with the oil lamp, a kind of night light. He pushed this door open further, finding it very heavy, and it swung back against his hand; so he held it open with his foot and looked round the door—to see a girl lying on a narrow bed.

.   .   .   .

Caroline seemed to be asleep, like her mother—and her father, now.

His heart began to thump.

There was just the slight sound of Caroline's breathing, and of his; and, suddenly, the hum of a car engine. Would this be one of the Leonis? The car went by. He put on the electric light in this room, and the child stirred. She was remarkably like her mother, and yet there was also a likeness to her father, especially about the eyes. Her eyelids fluttered; obviously she was near the surface of sleep, and it seemed to be a natural sleep.

Then Rollison saw the note on the bed, pinned close to the pillow, where he could not fail to see it. There was his name, pencilled—*the Toff*. There was a crude little pencilled drawing of the man without a face, too, as if whoever had sketched this had wanted to make a fool of him. That was what he had to remember: the Leonis would plan to make a fool of him. No matter how genuine

F*

this set-up seemed, it was not; there was some snag which he could not yet understand, some mystery which was unexplained.

It was too easy.

He picked up the note, and remembered the cards which he had picked up last night. He tore open the envelope, not worrying about fingerprints this time, and saw another card fall out. He picked it up. The child stirred again, but he did not glance at her. He turned the card over, and read:

"Leave the stones inside the bed when you've taken her."

He put the card back into the envelope, and tucked that into his inside coat pocket. The gun against his side seemed very heavy, but he had no immediate sense of danger, only of bewilderment. The Leonis would not make a fair exchange; there was no possibility of that. Still less would they accept diamonds without being sure of their genuineness. It was uncanny.

He pushed the bedclothes back.

Caroline stirred but did not wake. She was dressed in a pale pink nightdress and a quilted dressing-gown. The hems were rucked up about her knees, and her legs and feet looked very slim and pale. He hoisted her up, and she was a dead weight in his arms. He knew then that he dare not take any avoidable risk with her, and he placed the genuine diamonds in the bed, pulled up a blanket awkwardly, and wrapped it round her, and then turned towards the door.

It was still unbelievable, but no one moved, and there was no sound.

He went to the front door. The key was in the lock, but it was not bolted. He opened it. A car in the distance showed him up vaguely, and light shone on the face of the girl, who had snuggled down, as if glad of his chest to rest against. The light became brighter, and Rollison turned so that the driver of the car could not see what he was carrying. For a moment he thought that it was going to slow down; that it might be Leoni in the M.G.

It passed.

Rollison carried the girl to the Rolls-Bentley, opened the back door clumsily, and gradually pushed Caroline in. There was almost room for her to lie at full length, with her head against one corner. The courtesy light in the roof showed regular features, the wide-set eyes, the curling lashes, and the wavy auburn hair. He closed the door, and took the wheel. The obvious thing was to take her back to the school; she would be properly looked after there, and if she went straight back into school life and school atmosphere, the kidnapping might have much less effect on her. He started off. There was ample room to turn the car towards Hapley. He could still not believe that this had really happened, and that he had Caroline.

"*It's too easy,*" he told himself aloud. And then the thought flashed into his mind: 'They wouldn't let me have her *unless they believed they could get her back whenever they wanted.*'

That was it; they dared not let her go alive, but they had; so this was a kind of confidence trick.

He did not drive fast, his mind was crammed with jostling thoughts, and the urgent need to see through this trick. It was just conceivable that the Leonis had decided that the best thing was to give her up; they might have feared that the risk would be too great if they went on, but that theory didn't square with anything he knew about them. Ralph Kane might be wrong in his judgments, because he was emotionally involved, but Grice wasn't. Grice wouldn't talk about anyone as he talked about the Leonis unless he knew the truth. And Leah wasn't emotionally involved; she was just frightened.

Why should they let him get away with this?

Why was Max so sure of himself? How could they get possession of Caroline again?

The car wasn't being followed, and the street lights of

Hapley showed up, a garish yellow ochre. The spire of a church showed clearly. He saw a sign pointing to the railway station, and that reminded him how small the town was. In a few minutes he could swing off the road and into the school grounds, into the sanctuary of the school where Miss Ellerby reigned, and Miss Abbott did what she was told, where Mrs Higgs bustled and disapproved, and where Higgs stayed in the background. Here, where it had begun, it could finish. And—

"My God!" he breathed.

He actually took his foot off the accelerator, because the thought that flashed into his mind startled him so much. He slowed down, and pulled into the side of the road. He was only a few hundred yards from the road off which the school grounds led, and he saw the dim lamplight shining on it; here was the scene of the accident to Jeff—who might still be alive.

Could the Leonis get Caroline back from here?

Then he remembered seeing a wide-eyed girl who had missed Caroline, dressed in a quilted dressing-gown like Caroline's—the kind that Caroline was wearing. But Caroline had been fully dressed, so the nightgown had been taken from here to the cottage.

He did not think he needed to know much more.

He saw a small car parked in the dark driveway of a house near the school; an M.G. sports model. He saw the head and shoulders of the driver outlined against a glow of light from the house beyond. He had no doubt that it was Max Leoni; and he had few doubts about anything else. He swung the car out, then turned it between the open gates of the school. There were the same yellow lights as there had been last night, but no one was about. He swung round, in front of Miss Ellerby's house. He sat for a moment, watching the side of the house, and he saw a shadowy figure appear from some shrubs—from the garden where the M.G. had been parked.

Max.

Rollison opened the door of the big car, and as he did so another shadowy figure appeared from the other side, and he recognised Higgs.

"Who do you want?" Higgs demanded in his subdued voice, and then he saw Rollison drawing the girl out of the car, and cried wildly:

"You've found her!"

"Ring Miss Ellerby's bell," Rollison said.

"She—she ought to go straight to Miss Abbott's house, she—" Higgs was stuttering with excitement.

"We'll take her to Miss Ellerby's first," Rollison said. He carried Caroline, who stirred in his arms and then snuggled down more comfortably as the front door opened. Light streamed out as he stepped on to the porch.

"He's found Carrie Kane!" cried Higgs.

Miss Ellerby, standing there like a busty Amazon, exclaimed: "No!" and came rushing forward, threatening almost to knock Rollison to one side. "Oh, dear God, you've found her! Thank God, thank God!" She stared into the girl's face, and something in her voice did what Rollison had failed to do: it woke Caroline, and the light shone on to her bright eyes. "Give her to me!" cried Miss Ellerby, almost sobbing. "Higgs! Go and tell Miss Abbott, then make sure that Caroline's bed is ready in the sick bay, and bring the carrying chair. *Hurry!*"

"Yes, ma'm!"

"I'll manage her," Rollison said, and carried Caroline into the big, high, barely-furnished room where he had been the previous night; with only Miss Ellerby in it, it seemed more empty than ever. There was the large settee, and he laid the girl on it, while Mrs Higgs came hurrying, her eyes bright and her face flushed with excitement. "Mrs Higgs, we've got her back, everything's all right." Miss Ellerby went down on one knee beside Caroline, who was looking at her as if dazed, clutched the girl's hands, and said: "Did they ill treat you, my dear?

Are you all right?" Then there was a pause, before she asked: "Do you want anything to eat or drink? Higgs! get some milk, and some biscuits. Hurry, there's a good soul."

Mrs Higgs hurried out.

Caroline was moistening her lips, as if she couldn't find her voice; if she wanted anything, it was water, but Rollison did not speak, only stared down at her, and watched the schoolmistress who had shown such forced composure the night before behaving with such uncharacteristic excitement now.

Rollison went to the telephone. At first, Miss Ellerby did not notice that, but she glanced round suddenly, jumped up, and asked sharply:

"What are you going to do?"

"I'm going to tell the police that she's safe," Rollison answered.

"There's no need—"

"Don't be absurd," Rollison said. "There's every need to make sure they know at once."

"No, there isn't," rejoined Miss Ellerby flatly. "What on earth is the matter with you? If you send for the police now they'll come and pester the life out of the child with their silly questions—it would be a wicked thing to do." She glanced down at Caroline, who looked bewildered, and whose eyes were still very heavy with sleep. "For heaven's sake have some sense, and leave it until she's asleep, at least. When she has had a night's rest will be time to ask her questions."

Caroline said something in a low-pitched voice, and it was difficult to catch the words.

"I'm all right, Miss Ellerby," she seemed to say.

"I'm the best judge of that," snapped Miss Ellerby, and glared at Rollison, showing far more feeling than she had all the previous night. "I forbid you to telephone the police. I shall send for matron at once, and if in her view the child needs a doctor, then I shall send for the resident doctor. I have no doubt that both she and matron will prescribe the same thing: sleep."

"But Miss Ellerby—" Caroline began.

Rollison spread his hands, resignedly.

"All right, I won't tell the police yet," he conceded. "But at least I must telephone the child's father."

"I see no objection to *that*," conceded Miss Ellerby, almost reluctantly, and then Mrs Higgs came bustling along. "Higgs, I want you to send for matron. Tell her—"

"I've told her already," Mrs Higgs said, and this time Miss Ellerby could find nothing to disapprove. Rollison lifted the telephone. He saw that the headmistress was watching him, as if to make sure he did not dial the police. In fact he dialled O, and when the exchange answered, gave his own London number. Caroline was trying to sit up, and the headmistress pushed a pillow behind her back.

"There's no need to worry and no need to say a word," Miss Ellerby said; that was an order.

Rollison heard the ringing sound.

"And your mother and father have been very anxious about you; but they will soon know there is nothing to worry about." Miss Ellerby was saying. "You have to put it behind you, as if it were a bad dream. A bad dream," she repeated, as if to herself, and she nodded her big head.

"This is the hestablishment of the *honor'ble* Richard Rolleeson," announced Percy Wrightson, in a tone which would have made Jolly break into a grin.

"Percy," Rollison said, "is Mr Kane there?" He pressed the receiver close against his ear to make sure that none of Percy's answers could seep out into the room. Percy said, with simple straightforwardness, that he, Mr Ar, had put the knockout drops in his, Mr Kane's, glass so how the flipping hell did he expect Kane to be awake?

Rollison smiled into the telephone, and said:

"Hallo, Kane! I've some good news for you."

"*Look, I just told you*—" Percy began.

"Your daughter is quite safe, and back at her school," Rollison said. "Yes, you can certainly come down to see her. I'm sure that Miss Ellerby won't mind."

"*Aggie, his nibs 'as gorn crackers,*" Percy said in a hoarse aside.

"That is, provided you come down straight away," Rollison went on. "If you leave it until the morning it might be too late." He saw Miss Ellerby raise her head sharply, and went on hurriedly: "Miss Ellerby thinks it would be unwise to talk to the child about it in the morning, that it would be better if Caroline were to think that it's simply been a bad dream."

"*Absolutely stark raving mad,*" Percy breathed.

"Keep it to yourself for the time being," Rollison said. "If you don't there's bound to be a lot of unwanted publicity, and Bill Grice couldn't stop it if it really got under way."

"*Now 'e's talking abaht some cove named Grice,*" Percy groaned, as if he could not listen to this for another moment. "*Mr Ar, would you kindly ... What's that?*" Aggie's voice sounded in the background, and there was another gentle sound, as if one or the other was breathing heavily. Then Wrightson came back on the line, his voice pitched high with excitement.

"You there, Mr Ar? The only Grice I know is the copper."

"Yes, that's right, Mr. Kane. I should certainly come straight away," Rollison said desperately. "Never mind Bill—"

"Do you really mean I've got to tell Superintendent *Grice* to send the police to the school? Is that what you're driving at?" demanded Wrightson, shrilly.

Thank God for his sharp mind!

"Yes, just as fast as you can," Rollison told him. "I'll be waiting, don't worry." He put down the receiver and wiped his forehead. A young woman came hurrying in, obviously the matron; she turned to Caroline with her

arms outstretched in a most unprofessional way, and then
stood back, took her wrist, and looked into her eyes.

"I don't think she needs the doctor," she announced.
"Higgs can carry her straight to the sick bay; she'll be
perfectly all right."

That was the moment when Rollison saw the shadow on
the wall; the shadow of a man who looked squat and
broad-shouldered. He did not come any nearer, but
obviously he was in the passage; as obviously it was Max
or his brother.

Then Higgs came hurrying in, ready to carry the child
away.

22

MAX GLOATS

HIGGS glanced up at Rollison from beneath shaggy grey eyebrows, as Rollison eased the girl up for him to lift her more easily. The shadow remained at the doorway. Rollison stood back, looking at Caroline, seeing how sleepy and dazed she still was, wishing that he could keep her here, yet knowing that the next few minutes might be deadly, and that she must not realise that.

As Higgs took her towards the door, she said to Rollison: "Thank you very much for telephoning my father."

"I'm glad I could," Rollison said. "Don't worry about anything now."

"I won't," Caroline promised.

"Now stop this talking, Caroline, it's past time you went to bed," Miss Ellerby said, and bustled the child and Higgs out. The matron had already gone, and for a few seconds Rollison was alone in the room. He sat on the arm of a large arm-chair, watching the unmoving shadow in the doorway, and wondering how long it would be before Max revealed himself. Once the footsteps had died down, there was no sound at all. The scraping of a match as Rollison lit a cigarette seemed very loud.

His heart was thumping with the shock of his discoveries and the belief that he knew the whole explanation now; and the fear that Max, realising that, would make sure that he did not live to tell others.

He heard a car turn into the drive. The shadow moved. He wondered how long the police would be. First, Percy had to telephone the Yard, then the Yard had to contact the local police, and there was no certainty that the unimaginative Dawson would move really quickly; but he might. Rollison felt as if he were suffocating as he heard the car pull up close to the front door; the clearness of the sounds told him that the door was open.

Max's shadow moved.

A car door slammed and there were footsteps on the gravel; then a man called out:

"Is it okay, Max?"

"Yes, it's okay," Max called. "It couldn't be better."

The newcomer came briskly along the passage and, at the same time, the shadow of the other man moved. Then the Leoni brothers appeared in the doorway at the same moment, almost as if they were putting on a cabaret act. They looked a little theatrical, too, with the matching coats and wide shoulders, narrow trousers, with knife edge creases, the general immaculateness. Together, there was a likeness, but they could not be mistaken for each other; a mistake could only arise if one followed their descriptions, because words would make them sound almost identical. In fact, Felix was a little larger, and when he took off his stiff-brimmed trilby hat, grey hairs showed at his temples.

Rollison was on his feet, his right hand at his pocket, his expression suggesting that he was appalled as well as astounded to see them. Max had never had a brighter, broader grin, and he held an automatic.

"I shouldn't try to get your gun," he advised. "It was borrowed not long ago. You aren't very good, Toff, are you?" He glanced at Felix. "He even does our job for us, Felix. *Thank you for telephoning Ralph Kane.* We'll be very glad to see him."

Rollison said, hoarsely: "How did you get here? What are you doing—"

"Isn't he good?" jeered Max. "Would you believe a man could win the kind of reputation he has with that kind of a mind?"

"He hasn't had the right people to sharpen his wits on," Felix said.

"Shall we tell him everything?" asked Max, and then added as an afterthought: "Do you think he would die any happier if we did?"

"I wouldn't waste time," Felix said, and his tone and his expression told Rollison that he meant it; they had come to kill. They wanted to kill because of what he could tell the police; it was the only way they could make reasonably sure that they would be safe. Talk of the letter to the bank hadn't been enough to hold them back. He was quite certain that they did not intend to let him get away from here—as certain that they had no idea of the fact that he had sent that message to the Yard.

He needed ten minutes; or even fifteen. If he could stall them long enough, he might yet save himself; and Max's manner and sneers gave him the cue he wanted. He moistened his lips, backed away a pace, and he saw a glint in Max's eyes; but there was none in Felix's. Felix was the more coldblooded of the two.

"You–you don't need to kill me," he said, hoarsely. "You–you've got the diamonds. I left them there."

"That's right," Max said. "We collected them."

"Then I kept my part of the bargain!"

"That's right," said Max again, and looked marvellingly at his brother. "You hear that, Felix? He kept his share of the bargain." Again he mimicked, this time Rollison's voice, and it was surprisingly good. "The poor Toff thinks that because he plays to rule, everyone else does. You would think he was twenty-one, not forty-one or whatever he is."

"What are you saying?" Rollison demanded, and put a trembling hand to his lips, as if anxious to hide the fact that his lips were trembling, too. "There's no need to kill me, there was no need to come here. You–you've got forty thousand pounds and I–I've got the girl!"

Max laughed, explosively: and, for the first time, Felix smiled.

"So you've got the girl," Max mimicked again. "How wrong can a man be? *Jessie!*" He raised his voice and glanced at the door as he called out. "Jessie! Come and give Mr Rollison one of the shocks of his life."

There were footsteps; and then Miss Ellerby came in, looking as forthright and as massive as ever. She had a squarish mouth, and she was smiling rather tautly.

"Meet one of us," Max said.

"*Good God!*" gasped Rollison; but from the moment he had realised that the Leonis had let him find Caroline because they were so sure they could get her back, he had known the truth about this woman.

"No one will ever be able to say that you went out in a blaze of glory," Max sneered in his jubilation. "Our Jessie has been invaluable for years, haven't you, Jessie? Whenever we've wanted to hide one of our guests we've sent them along here to the sick room—and the resident doctor has turned a blind eye. It's surprising how quickly a woman will turn a blind eye if she makes enough out of it. You would be surprised how useful it has been to have such an innocuous cover for our nefarious activities," Max went on.

Rollison drew his hand across his forehead.

"I—I can't believe it."

"Hear that, Elly? You fooled him completely," Max said gloatingly, "and you'll go on fooling people for a long time. But not Rollison." He held the gun casually, but now Rollison was asking himself whether the man would kill him by shooting; it could be messy, and there would be the problem of disposing of the body. Then he realised that these men believed that they had all night to work in; they would probably take the body away and dump it—possibly at the cottage.

The obvious place was the cottage.

"Get it over," Felix said, as if he were bored. But Max wasn't bored; he was gloating over Rollison, and thoroughly enjoying seeing him so frightened; watching as he backed away, not realising that Rollison was edging himself into a position from which he could leap behind the couch, and so give himself some cover if shooting should start the moment the police cars arrived.

Surely the police wouldn't be long?

Outside, there was only the silence of the night.

"I wonder if he knows where Ralph Kane comes in," said Max, raising both of his eyebrows. "Do you think that would interest him, Felix?"

The older brother said: "You've had your fun, Maxie. We haven't all that time to spare. We want to get him back to the cottage, and we want to get the kid away from here again, before Kane arrives. We still need to keep a tight hold on Kane. Don't forget that."

"I suppose you're right," Max said, "but I like to see the Toff squirm. Where would you like it, Toff? Forehead? Heart? Belly?"

Rollison said chokily: "For God's sake don't shoot me! I–I've done everything I could. I've carried out my share of the bargain, I tell you. I–I'll back right out of the case, I won't look for the girl again. I've–I've done everything anyone could expect of me." He licked his lips, and his hands were raised a little in front of his face; for, if Max fired at his head, he might be able to take the bullet with his hand and deflect it. He spluttered as he pleaded, and the broadness of Max's grin, the taut smile on Felix's face, and the glint as of enjoyment on Miss Ellerby's told him how convincing this act was. "I'll forget everything I ever knew about you, I swear I will!"

"Just go down on your knees," Max ordered, "and plead with me that way."

"No! I—"

"Down on your *knees*, I said."

Then Rollison heard the engine of a car. It seemed a long way off. He listened for a split second, and thought that there was the sound of another car, and that both engines were moving fast. He went down on one knee. He saw Miss Ellerby turn away, as if in disgust; she muttered something that sounded like:

".... wouldn't have thought he was spineless."

Rollison was on his right knee—and the settee was on his right. There was a gap of three feet or more between it and the wall. If he could get in there with one diving movement, he could gain those few seconds that might be vital. Yet he dared not glance towards the settee, to measure the distance.

The cars were drawing nearer, and there was no doubt now that the drivers were in a hurry. Would these men realise why? Max was too delighted with his cat and mouse game, and even Felix seemed fascinated by the sight of Rollison on his knee, looking as if he were going to go down on both knees and place his hands together and plead—*pray*—for life. Rollison heard a car change gear, and knew that it was at the bend of the road.

Felix glanced at the window.

"Did you hear—"

Rollison dived towards the back of the settee, in a sideways movement. It seemed age-long as he scrambled between it and the wall, twisted round on his back, and then stretched up and pulled at the top of the settee; if he could bring it down on him, it would give him the seconds he needed. He heard the menacing report of a shot; he heard a twanging sound, as a bullet struck one of the springs. He saw Max appear over the top of the settee, gun in his hand, eyes burning as if gloating had turned in a moment to hatred. Max's weight was making it impossible to pull the settee down. Rollison buried his head in his hands and screwed himself up, heard the report of another bullet, felt a thud of pain in his right shoulder, and clenched his teeth as he waited for a third shot. It did did not come.

Men were running towards the house from the drive.

He heard a third shot, a long way off, but knew there

was no more danger for himself. He straightened out, and began to edge towards the end of the settee. His shoulder was already throbbing with pain, but he knew that it would not be long before he saw a doctor. He heard struggling, shouting, fighting. He got clear, gripped the arm of the settee with his free hand, and pulled himself to a standing position. He was wet with sweat, yet his mouth was parched.

Miss Ellerby was standing in a corner, terrified. Two plainclothes men were entering the room, and Max was reeling against the passage wall. There was no sign of Felix.

Then Superintendent Dawson came stalking in.

"Get to the sick bay," Rollison cried. "Make sure that no one hurts Caroline."

.   .   .   .   .

It was a needless fear.

The police found Caroline already sleeping in the sick room, the 'sanctuary' for so many helpless victims. Felix was caught in the grounds. The Higgses and the resident doctor were held within twenty minutes of the police arriving. Dawson, giving a little preliminary cough, asked earnestly:

"Is there any other information you can give us, Mr Rollison, on which to prepare charges? The only information I have is that you asked Scotland Yard for urgent assistance. These people assaulted some of my men, of course. I can hold them all, but if there are other charges . . ."

Rollison heard him out, and then said through the giddiness of pain:

"Dozens. Kidnapping, for instance. Holding a child to ransom. Demanding money with menaces. Attempted murder." He put a hand to his forehead, and for the first time Dawson saw that there was blood on it, and, also for the first time, Dawson actually sprang into action.

"You're hurt," he exclaimed. "You need a doctor. Sergeant! Telephone at once for Dr Millard. Mr Rollison, there is no need for you to exert yourself further, no need at all. I can take your statement later."

23

PARTING

It was half-past three the following afternoon when Rollison stepped out of the Rolls-Bentley, which had been driven by one of the Hapley police force, and went to his own front door. He was feeling rested and fairly fresh, although his right shoulder felt twice its usual size, and he had been told that it would be several weeks before he could use it properly; the shoulder blade had been chipped. He reached his own flat and Percy Wrightson gave him a beaming welcome, stood back, jerked his head towards the big room, and said in a gargantuan whisper:

"They're in there."

"Thanks, Percy," Rollison said.

Percy thrust open the big door, and Rollison went in. Kane was standing by the window, looking at him. Eve was moving towards the door from a chair near the Trophy Wall, hands outstretched. She gripped his left hand, and he saw the tears in her eyes; he also saw that she had a better colour, and that the drugged sleep had really helped her.

That—and the news.

"How is Caroline?" Rollison asked, and Eve said quietly:

"She's with my mother, Rolly. You were having that bullet taken out when I reached the school and they wouldn't let me see you."

"They were quite right," said Rollison, and glanced at Kane. Kane looked more rested, too, and more in control of himself—nothing like the man who would have shot and killed him. "Hallo, Kane."

Kane said: "I'll never be able to thank you, Rollison."

"Oh, forget it!"

"We won't forget it," Eve said, with a catch in her voice.

"Well, at least make sure that Caroline does," Rollison said. There was a pause, and then the rattle of crockery outside, and the door opened to admit Aggie Wrightson, carrying the best silver tray with the best silver teapot, the best china; everything which Jolly reserved for the really special occasions. And there were wafer-thin sandwiches, and a fruit cake; Mrs Wrightson meant to make sure that everything was done as it should be.

"Very glad to see you home, Mr Rollison," she said. "And isn't it good news about Mr Jolly? Did you know? Dr Welling says that he's out of danger."

"He told me this morning," Rollison said. "It's wonderful news. Thanks, Aggie."

She went out.

"Rollison," Kane said, "we all know that the school was used as a hiding place for missing girls, we know exactly how the kidnapping and the ransom was done, we know which of the members of the staff were involved, but—how much do you know about the rest?"

"Nothing," Rollison answered promptly, "but I can guess a lot."

"Guess, please," Eve said.

"If you'll pour the tea." Rollison watched her as she shifted the tray to a more convenient position, and was glad that there was this to occupy her while he talked. "Kane, how much have you told Eve?"

"Everything."

"Ah," said Rollison. "That's what I hoped. As for guessing—well, you often visit the places where the Leonis operate, don't you? You knew a great deal about them, and I didn't think it would affect you so much if you were simply going on what they'd told you; you knew all about them. And there was Leah. Eve always thought that Leah was just another *affaire*, but there were a lot of reasons for doubting that it was the whole truth. So I began to wonder what other hold she might have on you—and what other hold you were trying to break. That was fairly early on, soon after my mind began to work. I could understand the Leah I saw getting vicious with you, as a mistress, but I couldn't see her as a woman who would telephone Eve, and carry the war into your camp. There was something deeper, and—well, you acted for the Leonis for years, didn't you?"

Kane said huskily: "Yes. In a way."

"I haven't guessed what way," Rollison said quietly, and took his tea. "I needn't try, either."

Eve said: "You've got to know."

"I want you to know," Kane said, and waved his hands, "because—well, because we need your advice. The Leonis will talk to the police, of course—I'm surprised they haven't come to arrest me by now."

Rollison lifted his cup awkwardly.

"Did you keep them away?" Eve asked.

Rollison said: "I persuaded the police that if they would let Ralph Kane talk to me, I was more likely to get a completely unbiased story than if they started to question him right away. The police are always helpful when they can be. This time they know that it was Felix Leoni who ran their man Jeff down in the Hillman, which was used later to damage the car near Marple Guest House. They know it was Higgs who came to London and injured a man in Marple Street yesterday. They know they've got the two men who matter most under lock and key, and—well, the police are never vindictive. If you decide to turn Queen's Evidence you might find that things won't be too tough."

"I thought you would suggest that," Kane said. "It's almost a relief to know that you think they'd give me some consideration."

"They would give you a lot, if you told everything you

know," Rollison assured him, "It would have to be everything."

"Yes," Kane agreed, and repeated almost sharply: "Yes. I would never be able to live it down in this country, of course, but—" He seemed to square his shoulders, as if adjusting his mind to take whatever the future held. "It is very simple, Rollison. In the first place, I have always been—well, I will say highly susceptible. I have a certain presence and a way with young women particularly, and it was often easy to persuade one of them to come away with me. I have told Eve, and thank God she believes me, that I was never serious about them. It was a kind of compulsion, but you will hardly need me to explain that. The Leonis found out about this weakness of mine, and made certain propositions to me: that I should attract certain young women away from their families, ostensibly to elope with me, and leaving it to the Leonis to make a financial settlement. I take no pride in this, Rollison, but it is necessary to tell you the truth. The Leonis offered me money. The proposition revolted me, but I was badly in debt, chiefly through gambling. I hated the fact that I was poor and my wife was wealthy. I accepted two commissions, as one might say, thinking I could then back out. It was not easy, and I began to rationalise the situation. After all, the girls were old enough to know what they were doing, the parents were always wealthy, and, as far as I knew, nothing worse happened to the girls. But between the time of—er—a romantic attachment and being held to ransom, as it were, by the Leonis, one girl tried to escape and was found dead in France. The Leonis said that they could offer proof that I had strangled her. From then on I was inextricably involved. But when a few months later another girl was killed in the same way I told them that nothing would make me go on with this. They countered by threats against Eve, and Caroline, for they had come to rely on me a great deal. I did not know that Caroline's school had been used as a hiding place almost from the time that Caroline went there. With characteristic thoroughness, the Leonis found out about an old secret in Miss Ellerby's past—many years ago she was in prison, for fraud, under an assumed name. Any disclosure would have been ruinous to the school, and it is now obvious that Miss Ellerby co-operated most willingly, for a substantial consideration. The possibility of danger to Caroline terrified me. I warned Miss Ellerby to take especial care with her, having no idea of the futility of that, and told the Leonis that whatever the consequences, I would go to the police rather than continue to help them. I think it true to say that as my own daughter approached maturity, I realised more and more the nature of what I had been doing.

"The Leonis changed their tune, and I thought I had frightened them. They asked me to lie low while they finished a delicate negotiation with the parents of a girl whom I had known a few weeks ago. This was not unreasonable, and I was desperately anxious to avoid an open breach—I thought I might yet avoid any disclosures.

"So I stayed at the guest house, where I had often gone to see the Leonis." Kane looked wryly at his wife, and went on: "If I were wanted there, Leah Soloman would telephone me. Whenever I began to be difficult she would telephone Eve, and the Leonis would threaten to tell Eve the whole story. Leah didn't enjoy it, but she has always been completely dominated by Max Leoni, almost against her will. She was afraid Max would— would treat Caroline as he had so many others, and she knew how young Caroline was. Anyhow, I went to the guest house, believing that if I co-operated with the Leonis over this, the rest might work itself out. Then I was told they had kidnapped Caroline. I'd believed they were out of the country, and had been lulled into a completely false sense of security where Caroline was concerned.

"From then on, I dared make no move, for fear of what they would do to Caroline. I had to do what they told me—and I did so."

Kane stopped, at last, and it was a little while before Eve said:

"I think I know everything else, Rolly."

"Yes," said Rollison, and smiled reassuringly. "Everything that matters, anyhow. I haven't any doubt that you should turn Queen's Evidence, Kane. In fact, I think if I were you I would telephone the office of the Assistant Commissioner and say that you have a statement to make; that would get you off to a good start."

Kane said, slowly: "I will. Just one thing, Rollison."

"Yes?"

"How long a sentence do you think I'll get?"

"They'll have to charge you, and you'll get something," Rollison said. "It depends how good a lawyer you have, and how much you can convince the judge and jury that you acted under duress. I should say—" He hesitated, knowing that they were hanging on his words, and not anxious to be too optimistic or too pessimistic: "Three years, perhaps."

Eve exclaimed: "No more?"

"I would be surprised if it were much more."

Eve turned to look at her husband. He was staring at her, and there was a hint of a smile at his lips as he moved forward, put a hand on her shoulder, and then lifted the telephone from the desk, and began to dial. Rollison was looking at Eve, and he believed that she knew what was in his mind; that he had never looked upon a woman with greater longing. There was so much that he could have said, but nothing he must allow himself to say.

Kane finished dialling, and after a moment, said:

"I would like to speak to the Assistant Commissioner for Crime, please. I have a statement to make about the Leoni brothers . . ."

. . . .

Jolly came back from a month's convalescence a few days before the trial of the Leoni brothers, Miss Ellerby, Kane and the others began. During the trial, Rollison was at the Old Bailey most of the time, with Eve. On the last day, Caroline was with her mother, and when the judge passed sentence Kane was looking both at his wife and daughter, and hardly seemed to hear the words:

". . . and in view of your consistent efforts to simplify the work of the police and in view of the evidence that in some of the offences committed you acted under threat of violence I propose to be lenient and to sentence you to three years' imprisonment."

Eve and Caroline were looking at the man in the dock. Rollison doubted whether Eve realised who was sitting by her side. He knew and she knew that it would be folly to meet again; it would be best if he left her right away. So he went out of the court, and walked across London to Gresham Terrace, remembering that Joe Locket, Harry Mills, the Cartwrights and all of Ebbutt's friends would be looking eagerly for the sentences, and would rejoice at the life sentences which the Leoni brothers got, at the seven years for Miss Ellerby, and the lesser sentences on the others. He walked up to his flat, and Jolly opened the door, a plump, sun-bronzed and healthy looking Jolly, who murmured a greeting and thrust open the door of the big room, then went into his own quarters.

On the desk was a small packet, addressed to Rollison. He opened it. Inside there was tissue paper and, inside that, a lock of hair, companion to the lock which had been used to force Eve into compliance. And there was a card attached, reading simply: "*Thank you: from all of us.*" He picked up the lock of hair, took the other from his desk, and then examined the Trophy Wall, wondering where it was best to put this reminder not only of a case, but of a parting.